AN OFFER HE COULDN'T REFUSE

"I've got to warn you, this is a dirty, rotten job. The real danger is that the work will kill you inside. None of us have to worry about retirement because . . . okay, I'll level with you . . . none of us is going to live that long. I promise you terror for breakfast, pressure for lunch, tension for supper, and aggravation for sleep. Your vacations are the two minutes you're not looking over your shoulder for some hood to put one in the back of your head. Your bonuses are maybe five minutes when you're not figuring out how to kill someone or keep from getting killed. If you live six months, it'll be amazing. If you live a year, it'll be a miracle. That's what we have to offer you. What do you say?"

"Yeah, sure, sure," Remo said, "you can count on me."

The Destroyer #1

WARREN MURPHY & RICHARD SAPIR

CREATED, THE DESTROYER

PINNACLE BOOKS
WINDSOR PUBLISHING CORP.

PINNACLE BOOKS

are published by

Windsor Publishing Corp.
475 Park Avenue South
New York, NY 10016

Eighteenth printing: September, 1988

Printed in the United States of America

(Editor's Note: When we decided to reissue this book, we were told by Chiun, the Master of Sinanju whose exploits are described in this series, that he would write the foreword. We could find nobody to tell him no, and we dared not do otherwise.)

FOREWORD
By Chiun, the Reigning Master of Sinanju.

YOU READ LIES

Do not believe what you read in this book. It is too late for them now to set things right and you should not encourage these people to try.

This book is called a reissue which apparently is a new Pinnacle publishing word for a thin fabric of lies and distortions that is repeated at least once.

Do you know that when this alleged book was originally printed, it lacked even my picture? So now they make amends. Hah! Quick. Turn back. Look at the cover again. See? The pale piece of pig's ear shown there looks indisputably like my disciple, Remo. Notice the lines of weakness about the eyes. Notice the slobbering lips showing the creature's sloth. Notice the big white nose, a standard of ugliness to civilized people everywhere.

But, hold. Who is this Oriental on the cover? Who is that old man?

I know what these people are up to. They are trying to deceive you into believing that that is the countenance of the Master in an effort to trick some people into buying this compendium of literary duck droppings.

DO NOT BE FOOLED

That is not my picture. The face they portray is a cruel, hard, evil face. Where is the love, the kindness, the general sweetness that is my countenance? (To Pinnacle editors: "countenance" means what someone looks like.—Chiun.)

MORE LIES IN THIS BOOK

I appear briefly in this shoddy manuscript. The scribbler, Murphy, describes me as a karate teacher. To call the art of Sinanju karate is to call the noontime sun a flashlight. So much for Murphy.

I am going to tell you some things about this book. It is

called *Created, The Destroyer*. Everyone knows its real title is *Chiun Meets Pale Piece of Pig's Ear*.

And then they call the Masters of Sinanju killers. We are not killers but assassins. If America had competent assassins instead of amateur do-it-yourselfers, your civilization would be more orderly. But what can you expect of a country which would take off its beautiful daytime dreams to show fat men yelling about Gatewater? I will not forget them for that.

And another . . . oh, why bother? Trying to correct a typical Murphy set of mistakes is like trying to scoop out the ocean with a spoon.

CONGRATULATIONS

Fortunately, through a clerical error on the part of the scribbler, I have established my own following who receive bits of countervailing truth to stem this vicious propaganda. If you are among them, you are very lucky. You have perceived the goodness of this series, which is me.

But do not write to me at Pinnacle, for then you will expose yourself to all sorts of solicitation for various garbage which emanates from that publisher.

When you have Chiun, you need nothing else.

A FINAL DECEIT

Pinnacle Books has offered Murphy a chance to correct some of the errors in this pile of trash. I have warned him that he had better not: his perfidy should stand untouched through the ages as a demonstration of how low some men will sink just to enrich themselves.

Instead, out of the goodness of my heart, I offered to help set things straight with this foreword.

He said they would print it as I wrote it.

I do not trust these people.

Let them know now that I will read every word of these pages.

You are reading an English translation of my remarks. It is not as good as real language, but it is better than nothing.

When you are done with what I say, THROW THIS BOOK AWAY. It will do you no good.

With moderate tolerance for you,
I am forever,
Chiun
Master of Sinanju.

CHAPTER ONE

Everyone knew why Remo Williams was going to die. The chief of the Newark Police Department told his close friends Williams was a sacrifice to the civil rights groups.

"Who ever heard of a cop going to the chair . . . and for killing a dope-pusher? Maybe a suspension . . . maybe even dismissal . . . but the chair? If that punk had been white, Williams wouldn't get the chair."

To the press, the chief said: "It is a tragic incident. Williams always had a good record as a policeman."

But the reporters weren't fooled. They knew why Williams had to die. "He was crazy. Christ, you couldn't let that lunatic out in the streets again. How did he ever get on the force in the first place? Beats a man to a pulp, leaves him to die in an alley, drops his badge for evidence, then expects to get away with it by hollering 'frame-up.' Damn fool."

The defense attorney knew why his client lost. "That damned badge. We couldn't get around that evidence. Why wouldn't he admit he beat up that bum? Even so, the judge never should have given him the chair."

The judge was quite certain why he sentenced Williams to die. It was very simple. He was told to.

Not that he knew why he was told to. In certain circles, you don't ask questions about verdicts.

Only one man had no conception of why the sentence was so severe and so swift. And his wondering would stop at 11:35 o'clock that night. It wouldn't make any difference after that.

Remo Williams sat on the cot in his cell chain-smoking cigarettes. His light brown hair was shaved close at the temples where the guards would place the electrodes.

The gray trousers issued to all inmates at the State

5

Prison already had been slit nearly to the knees. The white socks were fresh and clean with the exception of gray spots from ashes he dropped. He had stopped using the ash tray the day before.

He simply threw the finished cigarette on the gray painted floor each time and watched its life burn out. It wouldn't even leave a mark, just burn out slowly, hardly noticeable.

The guards would eventually open the cell door and have an inmate clean up the butts. They would wait outside the cell, Remo between them, while the inmate swept.

And when Remo was returned, there would be no trace that he had ever smoked in there or that a cigarette had died on the floor.

He could leave nothing in the death cell that would remain. The cot was steel and had no paint in which to even scratch his initials. The mattress would be replaced if he ripped it.

He had no laces to tie anything anywhere. He couldn't even break the one light bulb above his head. It was protected by a steel-enmeshed glass plate.

He could break the ashtray. That he could do, if he wanted. He could scratch something in the white enameled sink with no stopper and one faucet.

But what would he inscribe? Advice? A note? To whom? For what? What would he tell them?

That you do your job, you're promoted, and one dark night they find a dead dope-pusher in an alley on your beat, and he's got your badge in his hand, and they don't give you a medal, they fall for the frame-up, and you get the chair.

It's you who winds up in the death house—the place you wanted to send so many men to, so many hoods, punks, killers, the liars, the pushers, the scum that preyed on society. And then the people, the right and the good you sweated for and risked your neck for, rise in their majesty and turn on you.

What do you do? All of a sudden, they're sending people to the chair—the judges who won't give death to the predators, but give it to the protectors.

You can't write that in a sink. So you light another cigarette and throw the burning butt on the floor and watch it burn. The smoke curls up and disappears before rising three feet. And then the butt goes out. But by that time, you have another one ready to light and another one ready to throw.

Remo Williams took the mentholated cigarette from his mouth, held it before his face where he could see the red ember feeding on that hint of mint, then tossed it on the floor.

He took a fresh cigarette from one of two packs at his side on the brown, scratchy-wool blanket. He looked up at the two guards whose backs were to him. He hadn't spoken to them since he entered Death Row two days ago.

They had never walked the morning hours on a beat looking at windows and waiting to be made detective. They had never been framed in an alley with a pusher, who as a corpse, didn't have the stuff on him.

They went home at night and they left the prison and the law behind them. They waited for their pensions and the winterized cottage in their fifth year. They were the clerks of law enforcement.

The law.

Williams looked at the freshly-lit cigarette in his hand and suddenly hated the mentholated taste that was like eating Vicks. He tore the filter off and tossed it on the floor. Then he put the ragged end of the cigarette between his lips and drew deeply.

He inhaled on the cigarette and lay back on the cot, blowing the smoke toward the seamless plaster ceiling that was as gray as the floor and the walls and the prospects of those guards out in the corridor.

He had strong, sharp, features and deepset brown eyes that crinkled at the edges, but not from laughter. Remo rarely laughed.

His body was hard, his chest deep, his hips perhaps a bit too wide for a man, but not too large for his powerful shoulders.

7

He had been the brick of the line in high school and murder on defense. And all of it hadn't been worth the shower water that carried the sweat down the drain.

So somebody scored.

Suddenly, Remo's facial muscles tightened and he sat up again. His eyes, focussed at no particular range, suddenly detected every line in the floor. He saw the sink and for the first time really saw the solid gray metal of the bars. He crushed out the cigarette with his toe.

Well, damn it, they didn't score . . . not through his slot. They never went through the middle of the line. And if he left only that, he left something.

Slowly, he leaned forward and reached for the burned-out butts on the floor.

One of the guards spoke. He was a tall man and his uniform was too tight around the shoulders. Remo vaguely remembered his name as Mike.

"It'll be cleaned," Mike said.

"No, I'll do it," Remo said. The words were slow in coming out. How long had it been since he had spoken?

"Do you want something to eat. . . ?" the guard's voice trailed off. He paused and looked down the corridor. "It's late, but we could get you something."

Remo shook his head. "I'll just finish cleaning up. How much time do I have?"

"About a half hour."

Remo did not answer. He wiped the ashes together with his big, square hands. If he had a mop, it would go better.

"Is there anything we can get you?" Mike asked.

Remo shook his head. "No thanks." He decided he liked the guard. "Want a cigarette?"

"No. I can't smoke here."

"Oh. Well, would you like the pack? I've got two packs."

"Couldn't take it, but thanks anyway."

"It must be a tough job you have," Remo lied.

The guard shrugged. "It's a job. You know. Not like pounding a beat. But we have to watch it anyhow."

"Yeah," Remo said and smiled. "A job's a job."

"Yeah," the guard said. There was silence, all the louder for having been broken once.

Remo tried to think of something to say but couldn't.

The guard spoke again. "The priest will be here in a while." It was almost a question.

Remo grimaced. "More power to him. I haven't been to church since I was an altar boy. Hell, every punk I arrest tells me he was an altar boy, even Protestants and Jews. Maybe they know something I don't. Maybe it helps. Yeah, I'll see the priest."

Remo stretched his legs and walked over to the bars where he rested his right hand. "It's a hell of a business, isn't it?"

The guard nodded, but both men took a step back from the bars.

The guard said: "I can get the priest now if you want."

"Sure," Remo said. "But in a minute. Wait."

The guard lowered his eyes. "There isn't much time."

"We have a few minutes."

"Okay. He'll be here anyway without us calling."

"It's routine?" The final insult. They would try to save his mortal soul because it was spelled out in the state's penal code.

"I don't know," he answered. "I've only been here two years. We haven't had anyone in that time. Look, I'll go see if he's ready."

"No, don't."

"I'll be back. Just to the end of the corridor."

"Sure, go ahead," Remo said. It wasn't worth arguing. "Take your time. I'm sorry."

CHAPTER TWO

It was a legend in the state prison that condemned men usually ate a heartier meal on the night of an execution than Warden Matthew Wesley Johnson did. Tonight was no exception.

The warden tried to concentrate on his evening paper. He propped it against the untouched dinner tray on his office desk. The air conditioner hummed. He would have to be at the electrocution. It was his job. Why the hell didn't the telephone ring?

Johnson looked to the window. Night boats moved slowly up the narrow black river toward the hundreds of piers and docks that dotted the nearby sea coast, their lights blinking codes and warnings to receivers who were rarely there.

He glanced at his watch. Only twenty-five minutes left. He went back to the Newark Evening News. The crime rate was rising, a front-page story warned. So what, he thought. It rises every year. Why keep putting it on the front page to get people worked up? Besides, we've got a solution to the crime problem now. We're going to execute all the cops. He thought of Remo Williams in the cell.

Long ago, he had decided it was the smell that bothered him. Not from his frozen roast beef dinner, untouched before him, but from the anticipation of the night. Maybe if it were cleaner. But there was the smell. Even with the exhaust fan, there was the smell. Flesh burning.

How many had it been in seventeen years? Seven men. Tonight would be eight. Johnson remembered every one of them. Why didn't the phone ring? Why didn't the governor call with a reprieve? Remo Williams was no thug. He was a cop, damn it, a cop.

Johnson turned to the inside pages of the paper, looking for crime news. Man charged with murder. He read through the story looking for details. Negro knifing in Jersey City. He would probably get the man. A bar fight. That would be dropped to manslaughter. No death sentence there. Good.

But here was Williams tonight. Johnson shook his head. What were the courts coming to? Were they panicked by these civil rights groups? Didn't they know that each sacrifice has to lead to a bigger sacrifice, until you have nothing left? Execute a cop for killing a punk? Was a decade of progress to be followed by a decade of vigilante law?

It had been three years since the last execution. He had thought things were changing. But the swiftness of Williams' indictment and trial, the quick rejection of his appeal, and now this poor man waiting in the death house.

Damn it. What did he need this job for? Johnson looked across his broad oak desk to a framed picture in the corner. Mary and the children. Where else could he get $24,000 a year? Served him right for backing political winners.

Why didn't the bastard phone with a pardon? How many men did they expect him to fry for $24,000?

The button lit up on his ivory telephone's private line. Relief spread across his broad Swedish features. He snatched the telephone to his ear. "Johnson here," he said.

"Good to catch you there, Matt," came the familiar voice over the phone.

Where the hell did you think I'd be, Johnson thought. He said: "Good to hear from you, Governor. You don't know how good."

"I'm sorry, Matt. There isn't going to be a pardon. Not even a stay."

"Oh," Johnson said; his free hand crumpled the newspaper.

"I'm calling for a favor, Matt."

"Sure, Governor, sure," Johnson said. He pushed the

11

newspaper from the edge of the desk toward the waste basket.

"In a few minutes, a Capuchin monk and his escort will be at the prison. He may be on his way to your office now. Let him talk to this what's-his-name, Williams, the one who's going to die. Let the other man witness the execution from the control panel."

"But there's very little visibility from the control panel," Johnson said.

"What the hell. Let him stay there anyhow."

"It's against regulations to allow . . ."

"Matt. C'mon. We're not kids anymore. Let him stay there." The Governor was no longer asking; he was telling. Johnson's eyes strayed toward the picture of his wife and children.

"And one more thing. This observer's from some kind of a private hospital. The State Department of Institutions has given them permission to have this Williams' body. Some kind of criminal-mind research, Doctor Frankenstein stuff. They'll have an ambulance there to pick it up. Leave word at the gate. They'll have written authorization from me."

Weariness settled over Warden Johnson.

"Okay, Governor. I'll see that it's done."

"Good, Matt. How're Mary and the kids?"

"Fine, Governor. Just fine."

"Well, give them my best. I'll be stopping down one of these days."

"Fine, Governor, fine."

The Governor hung up. Johnson looked at the phone in his hand. "Go to hell," he snarled and slammed it onto the cradle.

His profanity startled his secretary who had just slithered quietly into the office with the walk she usually reserved for walking past groups of prisoners.

"There's a priest and another man here," she said. "Should I bring them in?"

"No," Johnson said. "Have the priest taken down to see the prisoner, Williams. Have the other man escorted to the death house. I don't want to see them."

12

"What about our chaplain, warden? Isn't it strange to . . .?"

Johnson interrupted. "This whole damn business of being the state's executioner is strange, Miss Scanlon. Just do what I say."

He spun around in his chair to look at the air conditioner pumping cool, fresh, clean air into his office.

CHAPTER THREE

Remo Williams lay on his back, his eyes shut, his fingers drumming silently on his stomach. What was death anyway? Like sleep? He liked to sleep. Most people liked to sleep. Why fear death?

If he opened his eyes, he would see the cell. But in his personal darkness, he was free for a moment, free from the jail and the men who would kill him, free from the gray bars and the harsh overhead light. Darkness was peaceful.

He heard the soft rhythm of feet padding along the corridor, louder, louder, louder. Then they stopped. Voices mumbled, clothes rustled, keys tingled and then with a clack, the cell door opened. Remo blinked in the yellow light. A brown-robed monk clutching a black cross with a silver Christ stood inside the cell door waiting. The dark cowl shaded the monk's eyes. He held the crucifix in his right hand, the left apparently tucked beneath the folds of his robe.

The guard, stepping back from the cell door, said to Remo: "The priest."

Remo sat up on the cot, bringing his legs in front of him. His back was to the wall. The monk stood motionless.

"You've got five minutes, Father," the guard said. The key clicked again in the lock.

The monk nodded. Remo motioned to the empty space beside him on the cot.

"Thank you," the monk said. Holding the crucifix like a test tube he was afraid to spill, he sat down. His face was hard and lined. His blue eyes seemed to be judging Remo for a punch instead of salvation. Droplets of perspiration on his upper lip caught the light from the bulb.

"Do you want to be saved, my son?" he asked. It was rather loud for such a personal question.

"Sure," Remo said. "Who doesn't?"

"Good. Do you know how to examine your conscience, make an act of contrition?"

"Vaguely, Father. I . . ."

"I know, my son. God will help you."

"Yeah," Remo said without enthusiasm. If he got this over fast, maybe there'd be time for another cigarette.

"What are your sins?"

"I really don't know."

"We can start with violation of the Lord's commandment not to kill."

"I've not killed."

"How many men?"

"Including Vietnam?"

"No, Vietnam doesn't count."

"That wasn't killing, huh?"

"In war, killing is not a mortal sin."

"How about peace, when the State says you did, but you didn't? How about that?"

"Are you talking about your conviction?"

"Yes." Remo stared at his knees. This might go on all night.

"Well, in that case . . ."

"All right, Father. I confess it. I killed the man," Remo lied. His trousers, fresh gray twill, hadn't even had a chance to get worn at the knees.

Remo noticed that the monk's cowl was perfectly clean, spotlessly new too. Was that a smile on his face?

"Coveted anyone's property?"

"No."

"Stolen?"

"No."

"Impure actions?"

"Sex?"

"Yes."

"Sure. In thought and deed."

"How many times?"

15

Remo almost attempted an estimate. "I don't know. Enough."

The monk nodded. "Blasphemy, anger, pride, jealousy, gluttony?"

"No," Remo said, rather loudly.

The monk leaned forward. Remo could see tobacco stains on his teeth. The light subtle smell of expensive aftershave lotion wafted into his nostrils. The monk whispered: "You're a goddam liar."

Remo jumped back. His legs hit the floor. His hands moved up almost as if to ward off a blow. The priest remained leaning forward, motionless. And he was grinning. The priest was grinning. The guards couldn't see it because of the cowl, but Remo could. The state was playing its final joke on him: a tobacco-stained, grinning, swearing monk.

"Shhh," said the brown-robed man.

"You're no priest," Remo said.

"And you're not Dick Tracy. Keep your voice down. You want to save your soul or your ass?"

Remo stared at the crucifix, the silver Christ on the black cross and the black button at the feet.

A black button?

"Listen. We don't have much time," the man in the robe said. "You want to live?"

The word seemed to float from Remo's soul. "Sure."

"Get on your knees."

Remo went to the floor in one smooth motion. The cot level was at his chest, his chin before the robe's angular folds that indicated knees.

The crucifix came toward his head. He looked up at the silvery feet pierced by a silver nail. The man's hand was around Christ's gut.

"Pretend to kiss the feet. Yes. Closer. There's a black pill. Ease it off with your teeth. Go ahead, but don't bite into it."

Remo opened his mouth and closed his teeth around the black button beneath the silver feet. He saw the robes swirl as the man got up to block the guard's view. The pill came off. It was hard, probably plastic.

16

"Don't break the shell. Don't break the shell," the man hissed. "Stick it in the corner of your mouth. When they strap the helmet around your head so you can't move, bite into the pill hard and swallow the whole thing. Not before. Do you hear?"

Remo held the pill on his tongue. The man was no longer smiling.

Remo glared at him. Why were all the big decisions in his life forced on him when he didn't have time to think? He tongued the pill.

Poison? No point in that.

Spit it out? Then what?

Nothing to lose. Lose? He wasn't winning. Remo tried to taste the pill without letting it touch his teeth. No taste. The monk hovered over him. Remo nestled the pill under his tongue and said a very fast and very sincere prayer.

"Okay," he said.

"Time's up," the guard's voice boomed.

"God bless you my son," the monk said loudly, making the sign of the cross with the crucifix. Then, in a whisper, "See you later."

He padded from the cell, his head bowed, the crucifix before him and his left hand flinting steel. Steel? It was a hook.

Remo placed his right hand on the cot and got to his feet. The saliva seemed to gush into his mouth. He wanted to swallow bad. Hold down the pill. Under the tongue. Right where it is. Okay, now swallow . . . carefully.

"All right, Remo," the guard said. "Time to go."

The cell door was open, with one guard on each side. A large, blond man and the regular prison chaplain waited in the center of Death Row. The monk was gone. Remo swallowed once more, very carefully, clamped his tongue down over the pill and walked out to meet them.

CHAPTER FOUR

Harold Haines didn't like it. Four executions in seven years, and all of a sudden, the state had to send in electricians to monkey with the power box.

"A routine check," they had said. "You haven't used it for three years. We just want to make sure it'll work."

And now, it just didn't sound right. Haines' pale face tilted toward the head-high gray regulator panel as he turned a rheostat. Out of the corner of his eye, he glanced momentarily at the glass partition separating the control room from the chair room.

The generators moaned uphill to full strength. The harsh yellow lights dimmed slightly as the electricity drained into the chair room.

Haines shook his head and turned the juice back down. The generators resumed their low, malevolent hum, but just didn't sound right. Nothing was right about this execution. Was it the three-year layoff?

Haines adjusted his gray cotton uniform, starched to almost painful creases. This one was a cop. So Williams was a cop. So what?

Haines had seen four go in his chair and Williams would be his fifth. He'd sit in the chair too petrified to speak or move his bowels and then he'd look around. The brave ones did that, the ones who weren't afraid to open their eyes.

And Harold Haines would let him wait. He'd delay turning up the voltage until the warden looked angrily toward the control room. And then Harold Haines would help Williams by killing him.

"Something the matter?" came a voice.

Haines spun suddenly around as though a teacher had caught him playing with himself in the boys' room.

A short dark-haired man in a black suit, carrying a

18

gray metallic attache case, was standing beside the control panel.

"Something the matter?" the man repeated softly. "You look sort of excited. Flushed in the face."

"No," Haines snapped. "Who are you and what do you want here?"

The man smiled slightly, but did not move at the sharp question.

"The warden's office told you I was coming."

Haines nodded quickly. "Yeah, that's right, they did." He turned back to the control board to make the final check. "He'll be here in a minute," Haines said, glancing at the voltmeter. "It's not much of a view from where we are, but if you go to the glass partition, you can see fine."

"Thank you," the dark-haired man said, but made no move. He waited until Haines involved himself with his toys of death, then examined the steel rivets at the base of the generator cover. He counted to himself: "One, two, three, four . . . there it is."

He carefully set the attache case at the base of the panel where it touched the fifth rivet in the row. The rivet was brighter than the others, and for a good reason. It was not steel but magnesium.

The man glanced casually around the room, Haines, the ceiling, the glass, and when he seemed to be focussing on the death chair, his right leg imperceptibly pressed the attache case against the fifth rivet, which moved an eighth of an inch.

There was a faint click. The man moved away from the panel toward the glass partition.

Haines had not heard the click. He glanced up from the dials on the board. "You from the state?" he asked.

"Yes," the man said and appeared to be very busy watching the chair.

Two rooms away, Dr. Marlowe Phillips poured a stiff Scotch into a water glass, then put the whisky bottle back into the white medicine cabinet. Moments before, he had hung up the telephone. It had been the warden. He had almost shouted when the warden told him he would not have to perform an autopsy on Williams.

"Apparently, Williams has some unusual characteristics," the warden had told him. "Some research group wants his body. Don't ask me what it's all about. I'm damned if I know. But I didn't imagine you'd mind."

Mind? Phillips sniffed the beautiful alcohol aroma whispering comforting messages to his entire nervous system. He'd been prison doctor almost thirty years. He'd performed thirteen autopsies on electrocuted men. And he knew—no matter what the books said or the state said or his own knowledge and skill said—that it wasn't the chair that killed them, it was the autopsy knife.

The electric jolt numbed them, paralyzed them, destroyed their nervous systems and brought them to the edge of death. They would die. There was no saving them. But the autopsy, within minutes of the electrocution, really finished the job, he was convinced.

Dr. Phillips looked at the drink in his hand. It had started that way thirty years ago. His first autopsy and the "dead man" had twitched when the scalpel slipped into his flesh. It had never happened again, but it never had to. Dr. Phillips was convinced. And so it started. Just one drink to forget.

But not tonight. Just one drink to celebrate. I'm free. Let someone else kill the poor half-dead bastard, or let him die out his last few minutes in one piece. He gulped down the whisky and walked back toward the medicine cabinet.

The question stuck in his mind: what was unusual about Williams? His last physical had shown no irregularities, except for a high tolerance of pain and exceptionally fast reflexes. Other than that, he was perfectly normal.

But Dr. Phillips could not be bothered worrying about such trivia. He opened the medicine cabinet again and reached for the best medicine in the world.

It wasn't really a mile. It was too short for that. The whole damned corridor was too short. Remo walked behind the warden. He could feel the closeness of the guards behind him but he would not look at them. His mind was on the pill. He kept swallowing and swallowing, keeping the pill pressed beneath his tongue. He never knew he could create this much saliva.

His tongue was numb. He could barely feel the pill. Was it still there? He couldn't reach his hand in to find out for sure. Sure? What was sure? Maybe he should spit it out. Maybe if he could see it again. And if he saw it, what then? What would he do with it? Show it to the warden and ask him for an analysis? Maybe he could run to a drugstore in Newark, or take a plane to Paris and have it examined there? Yeah, that would be fine. Maybe the warden would go for that. And the guards. He'd take them all with him. What were there, three of them, four, five? A hundred? This was a whole state against him. The last door loomed ahead.

CHAPTER FIVE

Remo sat down in the chair by himself. He never thought he would. He kept his arms across his lap. Maybe they wouldn't electrocute him if they knew he'd never move his arms of his own accord. He wanted to urinate. A giant ceiling exhaust fan whirred noisily over his head.

There was a guard for each arm and they placed his arms on the chair arms and they strapped his arms to the chair arms with metallic straps and it surprised Remo that he let them do it as easily as if he wanted to help them. And he wanted to scream. But he didn't and he let them fasten his legs to the chair's legs with more straps.

And then he shut his eyes and rolled the pill beneath the left eye tooth which would be better for splitting it open.

He let them hinge a small metal half-helmet, resembling the network of straps from inside a football helmet, over his head. A band inside it pulled his forehead back against the back of the wooden chair. It was cold against his neck, cold as death.

And then Remo Williams bit into the pill hard, hard enough to crack his teeth and they didn't crack. And a sweet warm ooze filled his mouth and mingled with the saliva and he swallowed all the sweetness and shells that were in his mouth.

Then he became warm all over and drowsy and it didn't seem to matter anymore that they were going to kill him. So he opened his eyes and saw them standing there, the guards, the warden, and was it a minister or a priest? It certainly didn't look like the monk. Maybe it was. Maybe this was something they always did with executions: give a man the feeling that he had a chance so he'd go along willingly.

"Have you any last words . . . ?" Was it the warden's voice? Remo tried to shake his head, but it was locked to the chair. He couldn't move. Was it the pill or the straps that held him? Suddenly the question became fascinating. As soft, warm, darkness enveloped him, Remo decided he must look into the question someday. He would sleep until tomorrow.

Harold Haines, his visitor completely forgotten now, looked through the glass partition waiting for the warden to get angry. There were no reporters allowed at this one, and the few chairs in the room were empty. Tomorrow's papers would carry only a few paragraphs and the name of Harold Haines would not be mentioned. If reporters had been present, there would have been big stories telling about everything, even about the man who threw the switches, Harold Haines.

The warden wasn't moving. Neither was Williams. He seemed relaxed. Was he unconscious? His eyes were shut. His arms were limp. The bastard was out cold.

Well, Haines would wake him up, all right. There would be a gradual building of current, then the full force.

Haines was breathing hard now, a caressing, waking current, then slowly building to the climax and the final rush of juice into heaven. He could feel the heat of his own breath as the warden stepped back from the chair and nodded toward the control room. Haines slowly turned the twin rheostats. The generators hummed. Williams' body jolted upright in the seat. Haines eased off the rheostats slowly. He could already almost taste the faint sweet pork smell of burning flesh tickling the noses of those inside the room.

The warden nodded again. And Haines threw another jolt into Williams as the generators hummed.

The body twitched again, then sagged into the seat. Haines, gasping with a tremendous feeling of freedom, cut off the juice and let the generators die. It was all over.

He noticed his visitor was gone. He continued to throw switches shutting off the circuits. He was angered

23

by the bad manners of his visitors, the bad press coverage, the bad sound of the generators. Something, a lot of things, had been wrong. Tomorrow, he promised himself, he was going to take the whole control panel apart to see what was wrong with it.

Remo Williams' body sagged peacefully in the chair. His head, tilted toward one shoulder, clunked forward onto his chest as the guards freed his limp body from the bands. Dr. Phillips, who had come into the room after the electrocution was over, placed a stethoscope perfunctorily on Williams' chest, pronounced him dead, and left.

Attendants from the research center immediately got the warden's permission to move the body. They lifted Williams' corpse onto the wheeled stretcher gently, then covered him with a sheet. The guards thought the white-frocked attendants rather odd in the way they rushed moving the body as though the dead couldn't wait.

The attendants had placed Williams' hands rather formally across his belt buckle. But as they pushed the stretcher quickly down dark prison corridors, the hands slid loose and off the stretcher until his prone body looked like a diver entering the business part of a half-gainer. The attendants pushed the stretcher, its sheets barely trailing the ground, to a door opening onto a loading dock in the prison yard.

A new Buick ambulance waited there with open doors. The attendants lifted the wheeled stretcher into the ambulance, then shut the vehicle's doors, whose windows were blacked out. The windows on the sides were also blackened. Inside, the dark-haired man who had stood by Haines in the control room threw a blanket off his lap as soon as the doors clicked shut.

In his right hand, he held a hypodermic ready. With his left, he switched on an overhead light, then leaned over the body and ripped open the gray prison shirt. He felt carefully for the fifth rib, then sank the needle through the flesh into Remo's heart. Carefully, he pushed the plunger, slowly, evenly, until all the liquid

24

was emptied into Remo's body.

He withdrew the needle, careful to keep it on its entry path.

When it was out of the body, he tossed it toward a corner, then reached up to the ceiling and pulled down an oxygen mask on a tube. He could hear the hissing of the oxygen which started pumping the moment the mask was removed from its brace on the ceiling.

He pressed the mask over Remo's still pale face, then waited, staring at his watch. After a minute, he pressed his ear to Remo's chest. Slowly, a smile formed on his lips.

He straightened up, removed the mask, replaced it in its bracket, made sure the oxygen was off, then tapped on the window behind the driver's head.

The ambulance's motors coughed and the big Buick was on its way.

About fifteen miles from the prison, the ambulance stopped at a side road. One of the attendants, who had exchanged his white garb for a civilian suit, got out of the front seat and went over to a parked car against whose fender a man with a hook for a left hand leaned, casually smoking a cigarette.

The hooked man flipped the keys to the attendant, dropped his cigarette, then trotted to the rear of the ambulance. He rapped on the door and in an even tone, said: "MacCleary."

The doors flung open and he stepped into the vehicle in one smooth motion, almost like a large cat darting into a cave.

The dark-haired man shut the doors. MacCleary shuffled rapidly to a seat beside the body, still motionless on the black leather of the stretcher. MacCleary turned to the other man and said, "Well?"

"We got a winner, Conn," the dark-haired man said. "I think we got a winner."

"Nobody wins in this outfit," the man with the hook said. "Nobody wins."

CHAPTER SIX

The air in the ambulance tasted shot through with oral laxatives as the ambulance rolled along. "Probably the high oxygen content," MacCleary thought to himself.

He concentrated on the man on the raised stretcher in the middle of the ambulance and rejoiced at every up-and-down motion of the large chest covered by the sheet. This was the man. He might be the answer.

"Turn on the lights," MacCleary said.

"You sure, Conn? I was told no lights."

"The lights," MacCleary repeated. "Just for a minute."

The dark-haired man moved an arm and suddenly the confinement was bathed in a bright yellow glow. MacCleary blinked and then focussed on the face, the high cheekbones, the closed eyes, the lids that hid the deep brown orbs, the smooth white skin, marked by only a faint scar on the chin.

MacCleary blinked and MacCleary stared. He stared at the biggest pot he had ever been in on. It had violated every rule he had ever been taught about all the eggs in one basket. It was the wrong solution, but it was the only solution.

And, if the breathing human body on the stretcher worked, a lot more would work. A lot more people would live in a land they loved. The greatest nation on earth might survive as it has been intended to survive. And it might all rest with the slumbering body with the closed eyelids, glinting a shade darker in the bright light than the man's normal skin. Those eyelids. MacCleary had seen them before. And the light had shone on them then, too.

Only, it had been the sunlight, the hot Vietnam sun and the Marine had been sleeping underneath the wooden skeleton of a gray tree.

26

MacCleary had been in the CIA then. Dressed in Army fatigues, he had hiked up a hill with two Marines as escorts.

It was a back and forth stalemate time of the war. In a few months, he would be home. But right now, MacCleary had an assignment.

In a small village within American lines, a Viet Cong had set up headquarters. CIA's objective: enter main communications house and capture records, a list of major Viet Cong sympathizers in Saigon.

If the farmhouse, pinpointed as communications center for the VC, were attacked in normal fashion with men inching forward, the Commies could burn their lists of contacts. CIA wanted the lists.

MacCleary had worked out a plan to have a full company of Marines stage a charge on the building, with no one seeking cover, almost a Kamikaze attack. This, MacCleary hoped, would be fast enough to deny the time for record burning or anything else.

The Marines gave him a company. But when he approached the captain in command of the unit, the captain just nodded to a tarpaulin-covered pile on which two Marines sat, their M-1's cradled in their arms.

"What's that?" MacCleary asked.

"Your records," the captain said casually. He was a small, thin man who managed to keep his uniform pressed even in combat conditions.

"But the assault? You weren't supposed to start it before I got here."

"We didn't need you," the captain said. "Take your records and get your ass out of here. We've done our job."

MacCleary started to say something, then turned and walked to the tarpaulin. After 20 minutes of leafing through heavy parchments with Chinese lettering, MacCleary smiled and nodded his respects to the Marine captain.

"I will make a report expressing CIA gratitude," he said.

27

"You do that," the captain said sullenly.

MacCleary glanced at the farmhouse. Its dried mud walls were free of bullet pockmarks.

"How'd you go in? With bayonets?"

The captain pushed up his helmet with his right hand and scratched the hair over his temple. "Yes and no."

"What do you mean?"

"We got this guy. He does these things."

"What things?"

"Like this farmhouse deal. He does them."

"What?"

"He goes in and he kills the people. We use him for single-man assaults on positions, night-time work. He, uh, just produces, that's all. It's a lot easier than running up casualty lists."

"How does he do it?"

The captain shrugged. "I don't know. I never asked him. He just does it."

"I think he should get the Congressional Medal of Honor for this," MacCleary said.

"For what?" the captain asked. He looked confused.

"For getting these damn records by himself. For killing . . . how many men?"

"I think it was five in there." The captain still looked confused.

"For this and for killing five men."

"For that?"

"Certainly."

The captain shrugged his shoulders. "Williams does it all the time. I don't know what's so special about this time. If we make a big deal now, he'll be transferred out. Anyway, he doesn't like medals."

MacCleary stared at the captain, looking for the traces of a lie. There was none.

"Where is he?" MacCleary asked.

The captain nodded. "By that tree."

MacCleary saw that barrel chest in the crotch of the tree, a helmet pulled over a head. He glanced at the farmhouse, the bored captain and then back at the man under the tree.

28

"Keep a guard on those records," he said, then he walked slowly to the tree and stood over the sleeping Marine.

He kicked the helmet from the head with enough dexterity not to cause injury.

The Marine blinked, then lazily opened those eyelids.

"What's your name?" MacCleary asked.

"Who are you?"

"A major," MacCleary answered. He wore the leaves on his shoulders for convenience. He saw the Marine look at them.

"My name, sir, is Remo Williams," the Marine said, starting to rise.

"Stay there," MacCleary said. "You get the records?"

"Yes sir. Did I do anything wrong?"

"No. You thinking of making a career out of the Marines?"

"No, sir. My hitch is up in two months."

"What are you going to do when you get out?"

"Go back to the Newark Police Department and get fat behind a desk."

"It's a waste of a good man."

"Yes, sir."

"Ever think of joining the CIA?"

"No."

"Would you like to?"

"No."

"Won't change your mind?"

"No sir." The Marine was respectful with a sullenness that let MacCleary know the sirs were short convenient words just to avoid complication or involvement.

"That's Newark, New Jersey," MacCleary questioned. "Not Newark, Ohio?"

"Yes sir."

"Good job."

"Thank you, sir," the Marine had said and closed his eyes without bothering to reach for the helmet as a shade.

That had been the last time MacCleary had seen those lids shut. It was a long time ago. And it had been a long time since MacCleary had been with the CIA.

Williams slept just as peacefully under drugs. MacCleary nodded to the dark-haired man. "Okay, switch off the lights."

The sudden blackness was just as blinding as the brightness.

"Expensive son of a bitch, wasn't he?" MacCleary asked. "You did a good job."

"Thanks."

"Got a cigarette?"

"Don't you ever carry them?"

"Not when I'm with you," MacCleary said.

The two men laughed. And Remo Williams emitted a low groan.

"We got a winner," the dark-haired man said again.

"Yeah," MacCleary said. "His pain's just beginning."

The two men laughed again. Then MacCleary sat quietly smoking, watching the cigarette glow orange red every time he inhaled.

In a few minutes, the ambulance turned off the simple two-lane road onto the New Jersey Turnpike, a masterpiece of highway engineering and driving boredom. Several years before, it had had the best safety record in the United States, but the growing control of the road, its staff and the state police by politicians had turned it into one of the most dangerous high-speed highways in the world.

The ambulance roared on into the night. MacCleary bummed five more cigarettes before the driver slowed down and tapped on the window behind him.

"Yes?" MacCleary asked.

"Only a few more miles to Folcroft."

"Okay, keep going," MacCleary said. A lot of big shots were waiting for this package to arrive at Folcroft.

The journey was one hundred minutes old when the ambulance rolled off the paved road and its wheels

30

began kicking up gravel. The ambulance stopped and the man with the book jumped from the rear door of the ambulance. He looked around quickly. No one in sight. He faced toward the front of the big Buick. A high iron gate loomed overhead. the only entrance through high stone walls. Over the gate, a bronze sign glinted in the October moon. Its somber letters read: Folcroft.

Inside the ambulance, another groan.

And back at the prison, Harold Haines realized what had been wrong. The lights had not dimmed when Remo Williams had died.

At that moment, Remo Williams' "corpse" was rolling through the gates of Folcroft and Conrad MacCleary was thinking to himself: "We should put up a sign that says 'Abandon all hope, ye who enter here.'"

CHAPTER SEVEN

"He's already in Medical?" asked the lemon-faced man sitting behind the immaculate glass-topped desk, the silent Long Island Sound dark behind him, and the computer outlets waiting by his fingertips like metallic butlers of the mind.

"No, I left him lying on the lawn so he could die from exposure. That way we can finish the work of the state," growled MacCleary. He was drained, emptied by the numbing exhaustion of tension.

He had borne that tension for four months—from setting up the shooting in the Newark alley until last night's execution. And now, the unit chief, Harold W. Smith, the only other person at Folcroft who knew for whom everyone really worked, this son of a bitch with his account sheets and computers, was asking him whether he had looked after Remo Williams properly.

"You don't have to be so touchy, MacCleary. We've all been under a strain," Smith said. "We're still not out of the woods either. We don't even know if our new guest is going to work out. He's a whole new tactic for us, you know."

Smith had that wonderful way of explaining something you were fully aware of. He did it with such casualness and sincerity MacCleary wanted to break up the computer outlets with his hook and shred them over Smith's immaculate gray-vested suit. MacCleary, however, only nodded and said: "Do I tell him it will be only five years?"

"My, we are in a nasty mood today," Smith said in his usual professorial manner. But MacCleary knew he had gotten to him.

Five years. That was the original arrangement. Out of business in five years. That was what Smith had told him five years ago when they both resigned from the

Central Intelligence Agency.

Smith had been wearing that same damned gray vested suit. Which looked pretty damned peculiar because the two of them were on a motor launch ten miles east of Annapolis in the Atlantic.

"Five years should see this thing all wrapped up," Smith had said. "It's for the safety of the nation. If all goes well, the nation will never know we existed and the constitutional government will be safe. I do not know if the President authorized this. I have one contact whom you are not permitted to know. I am your contact. No one else. Everyone else is deaf, dumb and blind."

"Get to the point, Smitty," MacCleary said. He had never seen Smith so shaken.

"I chose you because you have no real ties to society. Divorced. No family. No prospects of ever starting one. And you are also, despite some odious character defects, a . . . well, a rather competent agent."

"Stop the crap. What are we doing?"

Smith stared across the foaming waves. "This country is in trouble," he said.

"We're always in some kind of trouble," MacCleary said.

Smith ignored him. "We can't handle crime. It's that simple. If we live within the constitution, we're losing all hope of parity with the criminals, or at least, the organized ones. The laws don't work. The thugs are winning."

"What's it to us?"

"It's our job. We're going to stop the thugs. The only other options are a police state or a complete breakdown. You and I are the third option.

"We're going under the name of CURE, a psychological research project sponsored by the Folcroft Foundation. But we are going to operate outside the law to break up organized crime. We're going to do everything, short of actual killing, to turn the tables. And then we disband."

33

"No killing?" MacCleary asked.

"None. They figure we're dangerous enough as it is. If we weren't so desperate in this country, you and I wouldn't be here."

MacCleary could see moisture well in Smith's eyes. So he loved his country. He had always wondered what moved Smith. Now he knew.

"No way, Smitty," MacCleary said. "I'm sorry."

"Why?"

"Because I can see the whole pack of us, everyone who knows about this CURE thing, being ferried out to some crappy island in the Pacific after we close shop. Anyone who knows anything about this is going to be dead. You think they're going to take a chance on you and me writing our memoirs? No way, Smitty. Well, not me, baby."

Smith stiffened. "You're already in. Sorry."

"No way."

"You know I can't let you out alive."

"Right now I can throw you overboard." MacCleary paused. "Don't you see, Smitty? It's started already. You kill me; I kill you. No killing, huh?"

"Internal staff is allowed. Security." His hand was busy in his jacket pocket.

"Five years?" MacCleary asked.

"Five years."

"You know I still believe that our bones are going to be bleaching on the sand on some Pacific island."

"There's that possibility. So let's keep casulties down in our section. Just me and you. Others do their jobs without knowing. Good enough?"

"And we used to laugh at Kamikazes," MacCleary said.

CHAPTER EIGHT

It was more than five years. CURE had found crime bigger, more organized than the strongest suspicions of Washington.

Whole industries, labor unions, police departments, even a state legislature were controlled by syndicates. Political campaigns cost money and crime had it. From the top came the word: "CURE to continue operations indefinitely."

Folcroft trained hundreds of agents, each knowing a special job, none knowing its purpose. Some were assigned to government agencies all over the country. Under the cover of FBI men or tax men or grain inspectors, they gathered up scraps of information.

A special section set up an informer network that plumbed careless words from gin mills, gambling dives, brothels. The agents were taught to use the fast five dollar bill or even the larger bribe. Bar flies, pimps, whores, even clerks at checkout counters unwittingly contributed to CURE as they picked up their small change from the guy on the block or the man in that office or that lady writing a book. A few words for a few bucks.

A bookie in Kansas City thought he was selling out to a rival syndicate when, for $30,000, he outlined how his bosses worked.

A pusher in San Diego who somehow was never convicted by the courts, despite numerous arrests, always kept a pocketful of dimes for the lengthy phone calls he would make from pay booths.

A bright young lawyer rose in a crooked New Orleans union as he kept winning cases until one day the FBI received a mysterious 300-page report that enabled the Justice Department to indict the leaders of the union. The bright young lawyer suddenly became very clumsy in court. The convicted union racketeers didn't get a chance for vengeance. The young man just left the state and disappeared.

A high police official in Boston got in over his head at the track. A wealthy suburbanite writing a novel lent him $40,000. All the young author wanted to know was which cop was on whose pad. Of course, he wouldn't mention names. But he needed them to get the feel of his work.

And behind it all was CURE. The information, in millions of words, the useless information, the big breaks, the false leads flooded into Folcroft, ostensibly headed for people who never were, for corporations that existed only on paper, for government agencies that never seemed to do government work.

At Folcroft, an army of clerks, most of them thinking they worked for the Internal Revenue Service, recorded the information on business deals, tax returns, agricultural reports, gambling, narcotics, on anything that might be tainted by crime and some of it that couldn't possibly be, they thought.

And the facts were fed into giant computers in one of the many off-limits sections of Folcroft's rolling grounds.

The computers did what no man could. They saw patterns emerging from apparently unrelated facts and through their circuits, the broad picture of crime in America grew before the eyes of the chiefs at Folcroft. The how of organized lawlessness began to unfold.

The FBI, Treasury Department and even the CIA received special reports, lucky leads. And CURE operated in different ways, where the law enforcement agencies were powerless. A Tuscaloosa crime kingpin suddenly got documented proof that a colleague, the man with whom he had split up Alabama's crime, was planning a takeover. The colleague got a mysterious tip

36

that the kingpin was planning to eliminate him. It ended in a war that both lost.

A large New Jersey pistol local changed command when sudden injections of big money saw the honest insurgents win at the union ballot boxes. It also saw the man who counted the votes retire quietly to Jamaica.

But the whole operation was slow, murderously slow. CURE made its strikes but no really finishing blows against the giant syndicates that continued to grow, prosper and stretch their money-powered tentacles into every phase of American life.

Moving agents into certain spheres—especially in the New York metropolitan area whose Cosa Nostra worked more smoothly and efficiently than any giant corporation—was like unleashing doves into a flock of hawks. Informants disappeared. A special division head of the informer network was murdered. His body was never found.

MacCleary learned to live with what he called "the monthlies." Like the agony of a woman's period would be Smith's every-thirty days berating.

"You spend enough money," he would say. "You use enough men and equipment. You spend more on tape recorders than the Army does on guns. And still the recruits you bring us don't do the job."

And MacCleary would give his usual answer. "Our hands are tied. We can't use force."

Smith would sneer. "In Europe, where you might recall we were highly successful against the Germans, we did not need force. The CIA uses very little force against the Russians and does rather well. But, you . . . you have to have cannons against these hoodlums."

"You know very well, sir, we're not dealing with hoodlums." MacCleary would start to boil. "And you know damn well we had armies following us in Europe against the Germans and a whole military establishment waiting against the Russians. And all we have here are these goddam computers."

37

Smith would straighten at his desk and imperiously command: "Computers would be good enough if we had the right personnel. Get us some people who know what they're doing."

Then he would make out his reports for upstairs, saying computers were not enough.

CHAPTER NINE

For five years, the routine was the same until two a.m. one spring morning when MacCleary was trying to put himself to sleep with his second pint of rye, and Smith rapped on the door to his Folcroft suite.

"Stay out," MacCleary yelled. "Whoever you are."

The door opened slowly and a hand snaked its way to the light switch. MacCleary sat in his shorts on a large purple pillow, cradling the bottle between his legs.

"Oh, it's you," he said to Smith who was dressed as though it were noon, in white shirt, striped tie and the eternal gray suit.

"How many gray suits you got, Smitty?"

"Seven. Sober up. It's important."

"Everything's important to you. Paper clips, carbon paper, dinner scraps." He watched Smith glance around the room at the assorted pornography in oils, photographs and sketches, the 8-foot high cabinet stacked with bottles of rye, the pillows scattered on the floor and finally to MacCleary's pink shorts.

"As you know, we've had problems in the New York City area. We have lost seven men without recovering even one body. As you know, we have a problem with a man named Maxwell whom we don't even have a line on."

"Really? That's interesting. I wondered what happened to all those people. Funny we didn't see them around."

"We're going to low profile in New York until we have our new unit ready."

"More fodder."

"Not this time." Smith shut the door behind him. "We've been given permission, highly selective but permission nevertheless, to use force. A license to kill."

MacCleary sat upright. He put down the bottle. "It's

about time. Just five men. That's all I need. First, we'll get your Maxwell. And then the whole country."

"There will be one man. You will recruit him this week and set up his training program in thirty days."

"You're out of your bloody mind." MacCleary jumped from the pillows and paced the room. "You're out of your goddam mind," he shouted. "One man?"

"Yes."

"How did you get us roped into that deal?"

"You know why we never had this type of personnel before. Upstairs was afraid. They're still afraid. But they figure one man can't do much harm and if he does, he's easily removable."

"They're damned right he won't do much harm. He won't do much good either. He won't make enough of a splash to wipe up. And when he gets it?"

"You recruit another."

"You mean we don't even have one on standby? We assume our man's indestructible?"

"We assume nothing."

"You don't need a man for that job," MacCleary snarled. "You need Captain Marvel. Dammit, Smitty." MacCleary picked up the bottle and then threw it against the wall. It hit something and did not break, only increasing his anger. "Dammit, Smitty. Do you know anything about killing? Do you?"

"I've been associated with these projects before."

"Do you know that out of fifty men, you might get one halfway competent agent for this type of work? One out of fifty. And I've got to get one out of one."

"Make sure you get a good one," was Smith's calm reply.

"Good? Oh, he'll have to be good. He'll have to be a gem."

"You'll have the finest training facilities for him. Your personnel budget is unlimited. You can have five . . . six instructors."

MacCleary propped himself on the couch, right on Smith's jacket. "Couldn't do it with less than twenty."

"Eight," Smith said.

"Fifteen."

"Nine."

"Eleven."

"Ten."

"Eleven," MacCleary insisted. "Body contact, motions, locks, armaments, conditions, codes, language, psychology. Couldn't do it with less than eleven instructors. All full time and then it would take at least six months."

"Eleven instructors and three months."

"Five months."

"All right, eleven men and five months," Smith said. "Do you know of any agent who would be suited for this? Anybody in the CIA?"

"Not the superman you want."

"How long to find one?"

"May never find one," MacCleary said, rummaging in the liquor cabinet. "Killers aren't made, they're born."

"Rubbish. Lots of men, clerks, shopkeepers, anybody turn into killers in war."

"They don't turn into killers, Smitty. They find out that they were killers. They were born that way. And what makes this damned thing so tough is that you don't always find them wearing guns. Sometimes, the really good ones have an aversion to violence. They avoid it. They know in their hearts, what they are, like the alky who takes one drink. They know what that drink means. It's the same with killing."

MacCleary stretched out on the couch and began opening a new bottle. He waved at Smith as if to dismiss him. "I'll try to find one."

The next morning, Smith was in his office drinking his fourth alka seltzer to wash down his third aspirin, when MacCleary entered with a bounce. He walked to the picture window and stared at the sound.

"What do you want?" Smith growled.

"I think I know our man."

"Who is he? What does he do?"

"I don't know. I saw him once in Vietnam."

41

"Get him," Smith said. "And you get out of here," he added as he popped another aspirin into his mouth. He called casually after MacCleary's back as he headed for the door: "Oh, there's a new wrinkle. One more little thing upstairs wants from your man." He spun toward the window. "The man we get cannot exist," he said.

MacCleary's grin evaporated into astonishment.

"He cannot exist," Smith repeated. "No one anyone can trace. He has to be a man who doesn't exist, for a job that doesn't exist, in an organization that doesn't exist."

He finally looked up. "Any questions?"

MacCleary started to say something, changed his mind, turned around and walked out.

It had taken four months. And now CURE had its man who didn't exist. He had died the night before in an electric chair.

CHAPTER TEN

The first thing Remo Williams saw was the grinning face of the monk looking down at him. Over the face glared a white light. Remo blinked. The face was still there, still grinning down at him.

"Looks like our baby's going to make it," said the monk-face.

Remo groaned. His limbs felt cold and leaden as though asleep for a thousand years. His wrists and ankles burned with pain where the electric straps had seared his flesh. His mouth was dry, his tongue like a sponge. Nausea swept up from his stomach and enveloped his brain. He thought he was vomiting but nothing came out.

The air smelled of ether. He was lying on some sort of a table. He turned his head to see where he was, then stifled a scream. His head felt nailed to the board and he had just ripped out part of his skull. Slowly he let his head return to the position where it had seemed to be punctured. Something yelled in his brain. His scorched temples screamed.

Kaboom. Kaboom. Kaboom. He shut his eyes and groaned again. He was breathing. Thank God, he was breathing. He was alive.

"We'll give him a sedative to ease the after effect," came another voice. "He'll be as good as new in a few days."

"And with no sedative, how long?" came the monk's voice.

"Five, six hours. But he's going to be in agony. With a sedative, he'll be able to . . ."

"No sedative." It was the monk's voice.

The puncture started moving around his skull, like a barber's hair massage with ten penny nails and kettle drums. Kaboom. Kaboom. Kaboom. Remo groaned again.

It seemed like years. But the nurse told him it had been only six hours since he had regained consciousness. His breathing was easy. His arms and legs felt warm and vibrant. The pain had begun to dull at his temples and wrists and ankles. He lay on a soft bed in a white room. The afternoon sun was coming through the one large window to his right. Outside a soft breeze rocked the color-gloried autumn trees. A chipmunk scampered across a wide, gravel path that no one seemed to use. Remo was hungry. He was alive, thank God, and he was hungry.

He rubbed his wrists, then turned to the stonefaced nurse sitting in a chair at the foot of his bed and said: "Do I get fed?"

"Not for forty-five minutes."

The nurse was about forty-five. Her face was hard and lined. She wore no wedding band on her man-like hands. But her breasts nicely filled out the white uniform. Her legs, crossed above the knee, could have belonged to a sixteen-year-old. Her firm backside, Remo thought, was just a hop out of bed away.

The nurse picked up a fashion magazine on her lap and began to read it in such a way that it hid her face. She fidgeted in the seat and uncrossed her legs. Then she crossed them again. Then she put down the magazine and stared out the window.

Remo adjusted his white night shirt and sat up in bed. He flexed his shoulders. It was the usual hospital room, white, one bed, one chair, one nurse, one bureau, one window. But the nurse wore no hat he recognized and the window was just one sheet of wired glass.

He twisted his right arm behind his neck and brought the back of his night shirt over his left shoulder. There was no label. He leaned back in bed to wait for food. He closed his eyes. The bed was soft. It was good to be alive. To be alive, to hear, to breathe, to feel, to smell. It was the only purpose of life: to live.

He was awakened by an argument. It was the monk with a hook versus the nurse and two men who appeared to be doctors.

"And I will not be responsible for this man's health if he eats anything but bland foods for two days," squealed one of the doctors. The nurse and the other doctor nodded approval in support of their colleague.

The monk was out of cowl. He wore a maroon sweater and brown chinos. The yelling seemed to bounce off him. He rested his hook on the edge of the metal bed. "And I say I'm not asking you to be responsible. I'm responsible. He'll eat like a human being."

"And die like a dog," the nurse interjected.

The priest grinned and chucked her under the chin with his hook. "You're cute, Rocky," he said. She whipped her face violently away.

"If that man eats anything but pablum, I'm going to Division Chief Smith," said the first doctor.

"And I'll go with him," said the second doctor.

The nurse nodded.

The monk said, "All right, you go. Right now." He began shooing them to the door. "Give Smitty my love."

When they were gone, he locked the door. Then he pulled a rolling tray from the kitchen over to the bed. He pulled over the nurse's chair and uncovered one of the silver vessels on the tray. It contained lobsters, four of them, oozing butter from their slit, red bellies.

"My name's Conn MacCleary," he said, spooning two lobsters into a plate and handing it to Remo.

Remo lifted a metal cracking device and broke the claws. He scooped out the rich white meat with a small fork, and swallowed without even chewing. He washed it down with a large draft of golden beer suddenly in front of him. Then he went to work on the lobster's mid-section.

"I suppose you're wondering why you're here," Remo heard MacCleary say.

Remo reached for the second lobster, this time crushing the claw with his hands, and sucking out the meat. A tumbler was half-filled with Scotch. He drank the smoky, brown liquid and quelled the burning with foaming beer.

"I suppose you're wondering why you're here," MacCleary repeated.

Remo dipped a white chunk of lobster meat into a vessel of liquid butter. He nodded to MacCleary, then lifted the dripping lobster meat above his head, catching the butter on his tongue as he lowered the morsel to his mouth.

MacCleary began to talk. He talked through bites of lobster, through the beer, and continued talking as the ash trays filled and the sun went down forcing him to turn on the lights.

He talked about Vietnam where a young Marine entered a farmhouse and killed five VC. He talked about death and life. He talked about CURE.

"I can't tell you who runs it from the top," MacCleary said.

Remo rolled the brandy over his tongue. He preferred a less sweet drink.

"But I'm your boss. You can't have a real love life, but there will be plenty of women at your disposal. Money? No question. Only one danger: if you get in a spot where you may talk. Then it's chips out of the game. But if you watch yourself, there should be no trouble. You'll live to a nice, ripe, pension."

MacCleary leaned back in the chair. "It's not impossible to live to a pension, either," he said, watching Remo search on the tray for something.

"Coffee?" Remo asked.

MacCleary opened the top of a tall carafe that kept its contents hot.

"But, I've got to warn you, this is a dirty, rotten job," MacCleary said, pouring a cup of steaming coffee for Williams. "The real danger is that the work will kill you inside. If you have a night free, you get bombed out of your mind to forget. None of us have to worry about retirement because . . . okay, I'll level with you . . . none of us is going to live that long. The pension jazz is just a load of crap.

He stared into Remo's cold gray eyes. He said: "I promise you terror for breakfast, pressure for lunch, tension for supper and aggravation for sleep. Your vacations are the two minutes you're not looking over your shoulder for some hood to put one in the back of your head. Your bonuses are maybe five minutes when you're not figuring out how to kill someone or keep from getting killed.

"But I promise you this." MacCleary lowered his voice. He stood up and rubbed his hook. "I promise you this. Some day, America may never need CURE, because of what we do. Maybe some day, kids we never had can walk down any dark street any time and maybe a junkie ward won't be their only end. Some day, Lexington won't be filled with fourteen-year-old hopheads who can't wait for another needle and young girls aren't whisked like cattle from one whorehouse to another.

"And maybe honest judges can sit behind clean benches and legislators won't take campaign funds from gamblers. And all union men will be fairly represented. We're fighting the fight the American people are too lazy to fight—maybe a fight they don't even want won."

MacCleary turned from Remo and went to the window. "If you live six months, it'll be amazing. If you live a year, it'll be a miracle. That's what we have to offer you."

Remo poured cream into the coffee until it was very light.

"What do you say?" he heard MacCleary ask. Remo glanced up and saw MacCleary's reflection in the window. His eyes were reddened, his face taut. "What do you say?" MacCleary repeated.

"Yeah, sure, sure," Remo said, sipping the coffee. "You can count on me." That seemed to satisfy the dumb cop.

"Did you frame me?" Remo asked.

"Yeah," MacCleary answered without emotion.

"You kill the guy?"

"Yeah."

"Good job," Remo said. As Remo inquired if there were any cigars, he wondered casually when MacCleary would find himself headed for an electric chair with a sudden absence of friends.

CHAPTER ELEVEN

"Impossible, sir," Smith cradled the special scrambler phone between his ear and the shoulder of his gray Brooks Brothers suit. With his free hands, he marked papers, setting up a vacation schedule.

A stiff, gloomy, rain whipped across Long Island Sound behind him bringing an unnaturally early nightfall.

"I appreciate your difficulties," Smith said, counting the days a computer clerk wanted near Christmas. "But we worked out a policy a long time ago about New York. No extensive operations."

"Yes, I know a Senate committee will be investigating crime. Yes. It will start in San Francisco. Yes. And move across the country and we will supply you with background and you will supply the Senate with background; yes, making the Senators look good. I see. Upstairs needs the Senate for many other things. Right. Yes. Good. Well, I'd like to help you, but no, not in New York. We just can't get a canvass. Maybe later. Tell upstairs, not in New York."

Smith hung up the receiver.

"Christmas," he mumbled. "Everyone's got to have Christmas off. Why not the sensible and convenient month of March? Christmas. Bah."

Smith felt good. He had just turned down a not-too-superior superior over the scrambler phone. Smith recreated the scene again for the pleasure of his mind: "I'd like to help, but no." How polite he was. How firm. How smooth. How wonderful. It was good to be Harold W. Smith the way he was Harold W. Smith.

He whistled an off-tune rendition of "Rudolph the Rednosed Reindeer" as he denied Christmas vacation after Christmas vacation.

The scrambler phone rang again. Smith answered

and casually sang: "Smith, 7-4-4." Suddenly he straightened, his left hand shot up to the receiver, his right adjusted his tie and he bleated out a snappy "Yes sir."

It was the voice with the unmistakable accent, giving the code number that no one needed to recognize him.

"But sir, in this area there are special problems . . . yes, I know you authorized a new type of personnel . . . yes sir, but he won't be ready for months . . . a canvass is almost impossible under . . . very good, sir, I appreciate your position. Yes sir. Very good, sir." Smith gently hung up the scrambler, the wide phone with the white dot on the receiver, and mumbled under his breath: "The damn bastard."

CHAPTER TWELVE

"What now?" Remo asked listlessly. He leaned against a set of parallel bars in a large, sunlit, gym. He wore a white costume with a white silk sash they told him was necessary in order to learn some things he couldn't pronounce.

He toyed with the sash and glanced at MacCleary who waited by an open door at the far end of the gym. A .38 police special dangled from the hook.

"One more minute," MacCleary called.

"I can't wait," Remo mumbled and ran a wicker sandal across the polished wood floor. It made a hiss and left a faint scratch that buffing would eliminate.

Remo suddenly sniffed the air. The scent of dying chrysanthemums tickled his nostrils. This wasn't a gym smell. It belonged to a Chinese whorehouse.

He didn't bother to figure it out. There were many things he gave up thinking about. It didn't pay to think. Not with this crew.

He whistled softly to himself and stared at the high wide ceiling buttressed by thick metal beams. What would it be now? More gun training? In two weeks, instructors had shown him everything from Mauser action rifles to pipe pistols. He had been responsible for taking them apart, putting them together, knowing where they could be jammed; knowing the ranges and the accuracy. And then there were the position exercises.

The lying down with your arm over a pistol, then grabbing and firing. The guarded sleep where your lids are half shut and you don't give yourself away by moving your body first. That had been painful. Every time his stomach muscles twitched as they do with anyone trying to move an arm to a certain position

51

while lying down, a thick stick would slap across his navel.

"The best way," an instructor had said cheerfully. "You really can't control your stomach muscles so we train them for you. We're not punishing you; we're punishing your muscles. They'll learn, even if you don't."

The muscles had learned.

And then the hello. For hours they had him practice the casual hello and the firing of the gun as the instructor moved to shake hands.

And over and over, the same words: "Get in close. Close, you idiot, close. You're not sending a telegram. Move your hand as if you're going to shake. No, no! The gun is obvious. You should have three shots off before anyone around you realizes you're hostile. Now try it again. No. With a smile. Try it again. Now with a little bounce to take the eyes off your hand. Ah, good. Once more."

It had become automatic. He had tried it on MacCleary once in a strategy session, those classes MacCleary chose to teach himself. Remo came in with the hello, but as he raised the blank pistol to fire, a blinding flash caught his eyes. He didn't know what had happened, not even when MacCleary, laughing, lifted him to his feet.

"You're learning," MacCleary had said.

"Yeah, it looks it. How come you noticed?"

"I didn't. My muscles did. You'll be taught that. Your reflex action is faster than your conscious action."

"Yeah," Remo said. "I can't wait." He rubbed his eyes. "What'd you hit me with?"

"Fingernails."

"What?"

"Fingernails." He extended his hand. "You see, I . . ."

"Never mind," Remo said and they got down to apartment entrances and locks. When the session was over, MacCleary asked, "Lonely?"

52

"No, it's a ball," Remo answered. "I go to classes. The instructor and me are the only ones there. I go to sleep and a guard wakes me up in the morning. I get up and a waitress brings me my food. They won't talk to me. They're afraid. I eat alone. I sleep alone. I live alone. Sometimes I wonder if the chair wouldn't have been better."

"Judge for yourself. You were in the chair. Did you enjoy it?"

"No. How'd you get me out anyway?"

"Easy. The pill was a drug to paralyze you into looking dead. We had the chair's electrical system rewired. When one of our guys pressed a switch, it cut the voltage down just enough to burn, but not to kill. After we left the place, a timer set the whole control panel afire so there'd be no traces. It was easy."

"Yeah, easy for you, but not for me."

"Don't knock it, you're here." MacCleary's constant smile disappeared. "But maybe you're right. The chair might have been better. This is a lonely business."

"You're telling me." Remo grunted a laugh. "Look. I'll be going out on assignments sometime. Why can't I go into town tonight?"

"Because when you pass that gate, you'll never return."

"That's no explanation."

"You can't afford to be seen near here. You know what happens if we're ever going to have to dump you."

Remo wished the blank gun strapped to his wrist were real. But then he probably couldn't get a shot off against MacCleary anyhow. Maybe just one night, one night into town, a few drinks. That was a modern lock but it had its weaknesses. What would they do to him? Kill him? They had too much invested. But then with this crew, who knew what the hell they'd do?

"You want a woman?" MacCleary asked.

"What kind, one of those ice cubes that cleans my room or delivers my food?"

"A woman," MacCleary said. "What do you care? Turn 'em upside down and they're all the same."

Remo agreed. And after it was over, he vowed it would be the last time he let CURE do his procuring for him.

Just before lunch, as he was washing his hands in the small bathroom attached to his room, there was a knock on the door.

"Come in," Remo yelled. He ran his hands under the cool water to rinse off the non-scented soap CURE had provided.

Drying his hands on the unmarked white towel, he stepped into the room. What he saw wasn't really bad at all.

She was in her late twenties, a few years younger than Remo. Athletically developed breasts pushed against her blue clerk's uniform. Her brown hair was set pony-tail fashion. The skirt swirled around her rather flattish hips. Her legs were just a bit thick.

"I saw your room number and the time on the board," she said. Remo recognized the accent as Southern California. At least, that's what he would have written on one of the speech recognition tests.

"On the board?" Remo asked. He stared at her eyes. There was something missing. They were blue, but deadened like lenses on small Japanese hand cameras.

"Yes, the board," she said, not moving from the door. "This is the right room?"

"Uh, yeah," Remo said, dropping the towel on the bed. "Yeah, sure."

Her face brightened with a smile. "I like to be undressed when I do it," she said, staring at his broad muscled chest. Remo unconsciously pulled in his stomach.

She shut the door behind her and before she reached the bed she was unbuttoning the blouse. She dropped the blouse over the wooden bedpost and forced her hands behind her back to unhitch the bra.

Her stomach was white and flat. Her breasts dropped gently from the bra's cups, but not so far as to show she wasn't firm. The nipples were red and already hardened.

54

She folded the bra over the blouse and turned to Remo and said, "C'mon, I don't have all day. I have to be back in codes in forty minutes. This is my lunch hour."

Remo forced his eyes away, then threw the towel off the bed. He dropped his trousers and his hesitancy.

She was waiting for him under the sheets by the time he unlaced his shoes. Gently he lifted the sheets and got into bed. She forced one of his arms behind her back, the other between her legs, and whispered, "Kiss my breasts."

It was over in five minutes. She responded with an animal fury strangely without honest passion. Then she was out of bed before Remo was really sure he had had a woman.

"You're all right," she said, wriggling into her white panties.

Remo laid on his back and stared at the white ceiling. His right arm was tucked between his head and the pillow. "How would you know? You weren't here long enough."

She laughed. "I wish we had more time. Maybe tonight."

"Yeah. Maybe." Remo said, "but I usually have instructions at night."

"What kind?"

"The usual."

Remo glanced up at the girl. She was putting her bra back on, Hollywood style. She held it in front of her, points down, then bent forward lowering her breasts into the cups.

She kept talking: "I didn't know what kind of work you do. I mean, I never saw a number like yours on the board before."

Remo cut her off. "What's this board you're talking about?" He stared at the ceiling. She smelled strongly of deodorant.

"Oh. In the recreation room. If you want relationships, you put your room and code number on the board. A man and a woman's number come up and

55

a clerk just matches them up. You're not supposed to know who you'll be doing it with. They say if you know you could get serious and everything. But after awhile, you can figure numbers and wait to put yours in. Like women always have a zero in front of their numbers, men have odd first numbers. You have nine. That's the first time I ever saw that."

"What's my number?"

"Nine-one. You mean you didn't know that? For crying out . . ."

"I forgot."

She chattered on. "It's a good system. The group leaders encourage it. Nobody gets involved and everybody is satisfied."

Remo glanced at her. She was dressed again and bounding toward the door in her low-heeled shoes. "Just a minute," Remo said, smirking. "Aren't you going to kiss me goodbye?"

"Kiss you?" she said just before she slammed the door. "I don't even know you."

Remo didn't know whether to laugh or just go to sleep and forget about it. He did neither. He vowed never to do his loving in Folcroft again.

That had been more than a week ago, and now he was anxious to get on with the assignments. Not that he relished the work. He just wanted to get out of Folcroft, get out of the cozy little jail.

He rammed the slipper against the gym floor again. There was probably some reason for slippers. There was a reason for everything. But he didn't give a damn anymore. "Well, how about it?" he yelled over to MacCleary.

"Just a minute now. Ah, here he comes."

When Remo looked up, he almost laughed. But the figure shuffling in was too pathetic for laughs. He was about five feet tall. A white uniform with a red sash hung loosely over his very skinny frame. A few white wisps of hair floated gently around his emaciated oriental face. The skin was wrinkled like old yellow parchment.

56

He wore slippers, too, and carried two thick boards that clapped hollowly with his shuffling gait.

MacCleary, almost deferentially, fell in behind the man. They stopped before Remo.

"Chiun, this is Remo Williams, your new student."

CHAPTER THIRTEEN

Chiun bowed. Remo just stared. "What's he going to teach me?"

"To kill," MacCleary said. "To be an indestructible, unstoppable, nearly invisible killing machine."

Remo threw his head toward the ceiling and exhaled loudly. "C'mon, Conn. Get off it. Who is he? What's his line?"

"Murder," MacCleary said calmly. "If he wanted, you would be dead now, before you could blink."

The chrysanthemum scent was strong. So it came from the Chink. Murder? He looked like an outpatient from an old age home.

"Want to shoot him?" MacCleary asked.

"Why should I? He's not long for this world anyway."

Chium remained impassive, as if he did not understand the conversation. The large hands folded over the thick wooden planking showed bulging veins. The face, even the slanted brown eyes, revealed nothing but eternal calm. It was almost a violent calm in the face of the recent offer. Remo glanced at MacCleary's dull gray revolver. Then he looked back into the eyes. Nothing.

"Let me see the .38." He removed the revolver from MacCleary's hook. It rested heavily in the palm of his hand. Remo's mind automatically rolled through the pistol qualifications as they had been drilled into him during training. Range, usual accuracy, percentage of misfires, impact. Chiun would be a dead man.

"Is Chan going to hide behind something, or what?" Remo asked. He spun the barrel. Dark shell casings. Probably extra primer.

"It's Chiun. And no, he'll be in the gym chasing you."

MacCleary's hook rested on his hip. It was a sign he had a joke in store. Remo had seen the "precede" several times before. They had trained him to look for the precede in every man. Everyone had it, the instructors said, you just had to learn to find it. The hook on the hip was MacCleary's.

"If I finish him, do I get a week out of here?"

"A night," MacCleary answered.

"So you think I might be able to do it?"

"No. I'm just stingy, Remo. Don't want you to get too excited."

"A night?"

"A night."

"Sure," Remo said, "I'll kill him." He kept the revolver close to his body, about chest high, where they taught him firing was most accurate and the gun safest from fast hands in front.

He aimed the barrel at Chiun's frail chest. The little man remained motionless. A faint smile seemed to gild his face.

"Now?" Remo asked.

"Give yourself a chance," MacCleary said. "Let him start at the other end of the gym. You'd be dead now before you pulled the trigger."

"How long does it take to pull a trigger? I have the initiator's advantage."

"No, you don't. Chiun can move between the time your brain decides to shoot and your finger moves on the trigger."

Remo backed away one step. His forefinger rested gently on the trigger. All .38's of this type had hair firing mechanisms. He lowered his gaze from Chiun's eyes to his chest. Perhaps it was by hypnosis through the eyes that Chiun could slow down his movements. One instructor had said some Orientals could do that.

"It's not hypnosis either, Remo," MacCleary said. "So you can look in his eyes. Chiun. Put down the boards. That'll come later."

Chiun lowered the boards to the floor. He was slow, yet his legs seemed to remain motionless as the trunk

59

descended to the floor. The boards made no sound as they touched the wooden floor. Chiun rose, then walked away toward the far corner of the gym where white cotton stuffed mats were hanging against the wall. As Chiun retreated, Remo's arm extended for accuracy. He did not have to keep the gun close to protect it.

The old man's white uniform was lighter than the mats. Still the coloring was no problem. The afternoon sun glinted off the red sash. Remo aimed just above it. He would go for the trunk and when Chiun was squirming in a blood puddle on the floor, Remo would take five steps closer and put two bullets into the white hair.

"Ready?" MacCleary yelled, stepping back from what would become the firing pattern.

"Ready," Remo called out. So MacCleary didn't bother to check the old man. Maybe this was one of the frequent tests. Maybe this old man, unable to speak English, pitiful in his frailty, was the victim offered to see if Remo would kill. What a pack of bastards.

Remo sighted by barrel instead of the "V". Never trust the sights on another man's gun. The distance was forty yards.

"Go," yelled MacCleary and Remo squeezed twice. Cotton chunks flew from the mats as the shots thunked where Chiun had been. But the old man was coming, moving quickly, sideways up the gym floor, like a dancer with a horrible itch, a funny little man on a funny little journey. End it now.

Another shot rang out in the gym. The funny little man kept coming, now crawling, now leaping, shuffling, but moving. Give him a lead. Crack!

And he kept coming. Fifty feet away. Wait for thirty. Now. Two shots reverberated through the gymnasium and the old man was suddenly walking slowly, with the shuffle with which he had entered the gym. There were no bullets left.

Remo in rage threw the pistol at Chiun's head. The old man seemed to pluck it from the air as if it were a butterfly. Remo didn't even see the hands move. The acrid fumes of spent powder drowned the scent of chrysanthemums as the old man handed the pistol back to Remo.

Remo took it and offered it to MacCleary. When the hook came close, Remo dropped the revolver to the floor. It landed with a cracking sound.

"Pick it up," MacCleary said.

"Stuff it."

MacCleary nodded to the old man. The next thing Remo knew, he was flat on the floor getting a close look at the grain of the gym's wooden flooring. It didn't even hurt, he went down so quickly.

"Well, Chiun?" Remo heard MacCleary ask.

In delicate, if not fragile, English, Chiun answered, "I like him." The voice was soft and high-pitched. Definitely oriental yet with clipped, British overtones. "He does not kill for the immature and foolish reasons. I see no patriotism or ideals, but good reasoning. He would have slain me for a night's entertainment. That is a good reason. He is a smarter man than you, Mr. MacCleary. I like him."

Remo got to his feet, bringing the gun with him. He didn't even know where he had been hit until he attempted a mock bow toward Chiun.

"Yeeow," Remo cried.

"Hold breath. Now bend," Chiun ordered.

Remo exhaled. The pain was gone. "All muscles, because they depend on the blood, depend on the oxygen," Chiun explained. "You will first learn to breathe."

"Yeah," Remo said, handing the revolver to MacCleary. "Say, Conn, what do you need me for if you've got him? I don't think you'd need anyone else."

"His skin, Remo. Chiun can almost disappear but he's not invisible. Can you hear witnesses saying they saw a yellow wisp of a man near every assignment we carry out? The papers would have a field day with the Phantom Oriental. And above all, Remo," MacCleary's voice dropped, "we don't exist. Not you, not me, not

Chiun, not Folcroft. Above an assignment, above our lives, this organization never was. Most of your assignments will be keeping it that way, I'm afraid. That's why it's especially important that you never make a friendship here."

Remo looked at Chiun. The brown slits remained impassive despite an obvious smile. MacCleary's head was bowed as if terribly interested in the boards at Chiun's feet.

"What are the boards for?" Remo asked.

MacCleary just grunted and turned from Remo and headed for the door. His blue loafers shuffled along in a gait similar to Chiun's. He did not shake hands or say goodbye. Remo would not see him again, until he had to kill him.

CHAPTER FOURTEEN

Harold Smith was eating lunch in his office when the direct scrambler line rang. It had little to distinguish it from the other two phones on the large mahogany desk, but a small white dot in the middle of the receiver handle.

Smith returned a spoonful of prune whip yogurt to the white porcelain dish on the silver tray. He wiped his mouth with a linen handkerchief as though expecting an important visitor, and picked up the receiver.

"Smith, 7-4-4," he said.

"Well," came the all-too-familiar voice.

"Well what, sir?"

"What about the canvass in New York?"

"Very little progress, I'm afraid, sir. We can't get past Maxwell."

Smith dropped the handkerchief to the tray and absently began to build prune whip yogurt drifts with the spoon. In the valley of tears that was his life, upstairs never failed to add a few thundershowers, then wonder why he got wet.

"What about the new-type personnel?"

"We're preparing a man now, sir."

"Now?" the voice came louder. "Preparing him? The Senate is coming to New York very soon, and it can't come with that Maxwell still operating. Too many witnesses disappear. We need a canvass, and if Maxwell's stopping it, then stop Maxwell."

Smith said "We only have an instructor-recruiter that's capable in this field . . ."

"Now, damn it. What the hell are you doing up there?"

"If we send our instructor, we'll only have the trainee."

"Send the trainee then."

"He wouldn't stand a chance."

"Then send your recruiter. I don't care how you do it."

"We need three more months. Our trainee will be ready then."

"You will eliminate Maxwell within one month. That is an order."

"Yes, sir," Smith said and hung up the receiver. He demolished the yogurt drifts and let the spoon sink into the grayish mixture.

MacCleary or Williams. One untrained, the other the only link to new material. Maybe Williams could pull it off. But if he failed, then no one. Smith stared at the white-dotted phone and then at the inter-Folcroft lines.

He picked up a local phone. "Special unit," he said into the receiver and waited. The noon sun sparkled on the waters of Long Island Sound.

"Special unit," a voice answered.

"Let me speak to . . ." Smith's voice tailed off. "Never mind," he said. Then he hung up and stared at the waters while he made his decision.

CHAPTER FIFTEEN

Remo had found Chiun's quarters much larger than his own, but stuffed with so much colored bric-a-brac that it looked like an over-crowded gift shop.

The elderly Oriental forced Remo to sit on a thin mat. There were no chairs and the table they ate from was ankle high. Chiun had said folded legs developed more tone than legs dangling from a chair.

For a week, Chiun only talked. There were no direct instructions on his trade. Chiun probed and Remo evaded. Chiun asked questions and Remo answered them with other questions.

Maybe the plastic surgery had slowed the pace of training. Surgeons straightened a break in Remo's nose and removed flesh from beneath the cheekbones to make them look higher. Electrolysis pushed back his hairline.

His face was still in bandages when, at one meal, he asked Chiun: "Ever eat a kosher hot dog?"

"Never," Chiun said. "And that is why I live so long." He went on: "And I hope you will never again eat kosher hot dogs or any of the filth you Westerners drop into your stomachs."

Remo shrugged and pushed away the lacquered black bowl that held the white, semi-transparent fish flesh. He knew that at night he could order real food.

"I see you will never give up your bad habits as far as your mouth goes."

"MacCleary drinks."

Chiun's face brightened as he lifted a sliver of the whitish fish. "Ah, MacCleary. There is a very special man. A very special man."

"You train him?"

"No, I did not. But a worthy acquaintance did. And he did an excellent job considering he was working with

65

a person of Mr. MacCleary's idealism. Very difficult. Fortunately, you will have no such problems."

Remo chewed on a few grains of rice that hadn't been tainted by touching the fish. A strange light filtered through the orange screens.

"I suppose I should not ask, but how did you escape the burden of this idealism?"

"You should not ask," Remo said. Maybe he'd get the prime ribs tonight.

Chiun nodded. "So. Excuse the prying but I must know my pupil."

Suddenly Remo realized the last nibble of rice had touched the fish. He would have spit it out, but he had done that the day before and Chiun had launched into a lecture on the preciousness of food. It had lasted half an hour, thirty minutes of tedium. Remo swallowed.

"I must know my pupil," Chiun repeated.

"Look, I've been here six days and all we do is talk. Can we get on with what we have to do? I know about Oriental patience. But I don't have it."

"In due time, in due time. How did you escape it?" Chiun began to chew the fish and Remo knew there would be at least three minutes of mastication.

"You assume I once had this idealism."

Chiun nodded, still chewing.

"Okay," Remo said softly. "I was a team man all my life and the only thing it ever got me was the electric chair. They were going to burn me. I went for a deal and when I woke up, it felt like Hell. I'm here and so's this fish and it is Hell. That's it. Okay?"

When Chiun had finished chewing, he said: "I see, I see. But one experience does not kill a thought. The thought remains. It is only hidden. It is a good time for you to learn. But when the feelings of your childhood return, beware."

"I'll remember that," Remo said. Maybe a steak would be better than prime ribs.

Chiun bowed slightly and said, "Remove the food. We begin."

As Remo brought the bowls to the sink painted with

66

purple and green flowers around the basin, Chiun murmured. He closed his eyes and lifted his head as though staring at a dark heaven.

"I am supposed to teach you how to kill. This would be very simple if killing were simply walking up to your victim and striking him. But it is not always that way in your trade. You will find it more difficult and complex and so your training will be more difficult and complex.

"Unfortunately, it takes many years to build an expert. And I do not have many years in which to train you. Once I was given a man from your Central Intelligence Agency and told to train him in two weeks for a European assignment. I pleaded that this was not enough time; that he was not ready. They would not listen. And he lived but two weeks. It is pitiful that there is not more central intelligence in your Central Intelligence Agency.

"They have, however, promised me more time with you. How much more, neither of us know. We will try to learn as much as we can in these first few weeks, and then we can return, if time remains, to the beginning and specialize.

"Before you can learn anything, you must know what you are studying. All the defense arts are an application of Zen beliefs."

Remo smiled.

"You know Zen?" Chiun asked.

"Sure. Beards and bums and black coffee."

Chiun frowned. "Theirs is not Zen; theirs is nonsense."

"You will see," he continued. "All the defense arts . . . *judo, karate, king fu, aiki* . . . are based upon the philosophy of instant action when action is required. But that action must be instinctive, not learned. It must proceed naturally from the person, from his being. It is not your coat, which you can remove, but your skin, which you cannot. It may sound very complex, Mr. Remo, but it will become more clear.

"Most important to all your training will be your breathing."

"Of course," Remo said dryly.

Chiun ignored the joke.

"If you do not learn to breathe properly, you will learn to do nothing properly. This is most important and you must practice correct breathing until it becomes instinctive. Ordinarily, further training would await that time. Under these conditions, it cannot."

He rose and went to a black lacquered cabinet from which he removed a black metal metronome. He placed it on the table between himself and Remo.

For Remo, there followed the most boring afternoon of his life. Chiun explained different breathing techniques, and recommended a course of two beats inhale, two beats hold breath, two beats exhale for Remo.

Remo practiced it all afternoon as the metronome clicked and Chiun talked. He caught only parts of what the old Oriental was saying: the *ki-ai*, spirit breath, welding your breath with that of the universal in order to weld the universal's power to your power.

Press down the breath, Chiun exhorted. Pull it down into your groin, down in behind the complex of nerves that control the emotions . . . down, down, down.

Calm those nerves. Calm nerves make a calm man and a calm man feels no fear. As you breathe, meditate. Clear your mind of thoughts and impressions from outside you. Then the thing inside you . . . your mission . . . can receive all your attention.

He went on and on into the evening. Then he told Remo: "You do very well. And already you walk well. Balance and breathing. There is little else. Tomorrow we specialize."

The next morning Chiun explained the difference between the self-defense arts: the difference between a "*do*," a way; and a "*jitsu*," a technique.

"You have learned *judo* in the military," Chiun said as a half-question.

Remo nodded. Chiun frowned. "There is much then to unlearn."

"You have learned to fall?" he asked.

Remo nodded, recalling the *judo* falling technique of hit, roll and slap with your arm to dissipate the force of the fall.

"Forget it," Chiun said. "Instead of falling like the dummy, we learn to fall like the dishcloth."

They moved out toward the mats on the gymnasium floor. "This is *aiki-do*, Mr. Williams," he said. "It is a defense art pure and simple. The art of escaping, not being hurt and coming back to fight. *Judo* is a system of straight lines; in *aiki* we would emulate the circle. Throw me over your shoulder, Mr. Williams."

Remo moved around in front of Chiun, grabbed his arm and tossed the tiny little man over his shoulder. *Judo* technique would call for Chiun to hit the mats, roll, and slap out with his arm to nullify the force of the fall. Instead, he hit like a ball, rolled, spun and ended on his feet facing Remo, all in one motion.

"This is what you must learn," Chiun said. "Now encircle me from behind."

Remo moved up behind Chiun, then grabbed him around the chest, pinning his arms to his sides.

In *judo*, there are many responses to this attack, all of them violent. Smash the head back into the face of your attacker; twist your body to the side and drive your elbow into your attacker's throat; stamp onto your opponent's instep; bend down and grab your assailant's ankles through your legs, pull up and smash back into his stomach.

Chiun tried none of them.

Remo perversely began to apply more pressure. He felt Chiun wince and his muscles tighten. Chiun reached up and placed one hand on each of Remo's wrists. With steady, even pressure, he simply pulled Remo's hands apart . . . an inch . . . two inches . . . until finally they broke apart. Chiun spun, came up under Remo's armpit, and flashed him over his back into a pile at the edge of the mat.

Remo sat there, dazed.

Chiun said: "You forgot to roll."

Remo rose slowly. "How the hell did you do that?

Christ knows I'm stronger than you."

"Yes, you are, but your strength is rarely directed from one point to another point. Instead it sprays out from your muscles in many directions. I simply concentrated my puny strength in the *saika tanden*, the abdomen's nerve center, and then directed it through my arms outward. I could pull apart ten men's hands that way, and you could do the same with twenty men, when you learn. And you will."

He continued the drill.

Three mornings later, Chiun told Remo: "You have had enough *aiki*. It is a defense art and you are not to be a defender. You are to learn attack. I have been told we have not much more time so we must hurry."

He led Remo to the pounding posts at the end of the gym. As they walked, he explained, "There are many types of offensive arts in the East and all are excellent if performed well. We must, however, concentrate on one and *karate* is by far the most versatile."

They stood within the rectangle made by the four shoulder-high Y-shaped posts.

Chiun continued: "The story is told of the beginning of *karate* that many years ago the peasants of a Chinese province were disarmed by their evil ruler. Dharma, who began the science of Zen, lived in that time. And he knew his people must be able to protect themselves. So he called them to a meeting."

Even as he spoke, Chiun was setting inch-thick pine blocks into the Y-shaped posts.

"Dharma told his people they must defend themselves. He said, 'We have lost our knives, so turn every finger into a knife'. . ." And with the points of his fingers, Chiun snaked out at one pine board. Its two halves dropped with a clunk on the floor.

"And Dharma said, 'We no longer have maces, so every fist must be a mace' . . ." and with his fist clenched, Chiun thumped out, splitting the board in the second Y-post.

Chiun stood before the third post. "Without spears, every arm must be a spear," he quoted, and he punched out stiff-armed, jolting the third block into two pieces. He stood there momentarily looking at the solid two-by-four Y-post from which the two halves of the board had fallen.

He inhaled deeply. "And Dharma said: 'Make every open hand into a sword!' . . ." The last words were almost shouted in a violent expulsion of air. And Chiun's open hand splashed forward, its side smacking against the two-by-four with a report like a rifle shot. And then the post wasn't there. It tumbled and fell, severed cleanly three feet from its base.

Chiun turned to Remo. "This is the art of the open hand, which we know as *karate* and carry on today. You will learn it."

Remo picked up the broken top section of two-by-four and looked at its splintered edge. He had to admit it. Chiun was impressive. What could stop this little man if he took a notion to kill? Who could fail to fall in front of those terrifying hands?

CHAPTER SIXTEEN

During the *aiki* training, Remo had been taught the body's main pressure points. There were hundreds of them, Chiun had told him, but only about sixty were of any practical value and only eight were reliable killers.

"These are the eight you will concentrate on," Chiun said.

After lunch, Remo found two life-size dummies mounted on spring bases in the gym. They wore the white gym uniforms, but had red spots painted at both temples, the adam's apple, the solar plexus, both kidneys, the base of the skull and a spot that he learned later was the seventh major vertebra.

"There is one *karate* hand formation. It is the basis of all others," Chiun began as they sat on the mats facing the dummies. He opened his hand, palm up, and extended all the fingers. "The thumb must be cocked," he said, "much as the hammer on a pistol. There should be a pulling motion extending back into your forearm. This, in turn," he continued, "results in an extension—a pushing forward—of your little finger. The three center fingers are slightly bent at the ends and the entire hand is slightly bowed."

He brought his hand into position. "Feel my forearm," he told Remo. Remo did. It was like braided rope.

"It is not exertion, but tension, that creates this toughness," Chiun said. "And it is not strength, but this tension, which makes the hand such a weapon."

He brought Remo to the dummies and began instructing him in dealing volleys of hand-chops . . . right, left; low, high; over and over.

Although the dummies were packed hard with rope fibers, Remo's hands were virtually immune from the impact, he found.

Once Chiun stopped him. "You are attempting to follow through with your blows. There is no follow-through in *karate*. Instead, a snapping motion is used."

He took a pack of paper matches from his pocket. "Light one, Mr. Remo," he said.

Remo lit it and held it at arm's length. Chiun faced it, lifted his hand up to shoulder level, then lashed downward with a strong exhaling. Just before his hand reached the flame, it reversed itself and snapped back up. The flame seemed to jump up after it, in the vacuum caused by Chiun's lightning move, and the match was out.

"That is the motion and action one must strive for," Chiun said.

"I don't want to put out fires. I want to break boards," Remo said. "When will I be able to do that?"

"You already can," Chiun said. "But first, the practice."

He kept Remo working on the dummies for hours. Toward evening, he showed him the other *karate* hand formations. The hand sword Remo had first been shown, he learned, was called *shuto*. It could be held all day without tiring.

Let the hand bend back slightly at the wrist. This is the hand piston—*shotei*—and is used for striking the chin or throat. The *hiraken* is made the same way, but the middle fingers bend more. It is a paddle . . . "very good for boxing ears and breaking eardrums," Chiun explained.

The mace, formed by rolling the hand sword into a fist, is called *tetsui*. "There are others, but these are the ones you will need to know," Chiun said.

"When you learn the art of extending your power through your hands and through your feet, you will learn, too, to extend it through inanimate objects. In the hands of an expert, all things are deadly weapons." He showed Remo how to make knives of paper and deadly darts of paper clips. How much more he could have shown Remo went unanswered. A guard entered Chiun's quarters at three o'clock one morning. He

73

spoke softly to Chiun for a few moments.

The old man bowed his head, then nodded to Remo who was awake but motionless.

"Follow him," he told his pupil.

Remo rose from the straw-thin sleeping mat and slipped into a pair of sandals. The guard seemed nervous. He apparently knew he was in one of the rooms of the special unit.

As Remo approached him he backed away toward the door. Remo nodded for him to lead the way.

The wind from the Sound ripped through Remo's thin white tunic as he walked behind the guard down one of the stone paths. The November moon cast an eerie light over the darkened buildings. Remo contained his breathing to limit the effect of the chill. But by the time he and the guard reached the main administrative hall, he was slapping his arms to keep warm.

The guard wore a thick wool jacket which he kept buttoned even as they entered the building and rode up two flights in the self-service elevator. They were stopped by two guards and Remo's man had to show his passes twice before they reached an oak door with a brass handle. Funny how Remo noticed the off-balance postures of the guards now. They held their hands almost inviting to be thrown.

Unconsciously, Remo had recorded that they would be easy to penetrate.

Lettering on the door read: "Private."

The guard stopped. "I can't enter here, sir."

Remo grunted acknowledgment and turned the brass handle. The door swung outward instead of into the room. By its inertia, Remo judged it couldn't be penetrated by a pistol shot, except perhaps from a .357 Magnum.

A thin man in a blue bathrobe leaned against a mahogany desk sipping from a white steaming cup. He was staring out at the darkness and the moon-splashed Sound.

Remo pulled the door shut behind him. A .357 wouldn't penetrate.

"I'm Smith," the man said without turning around. "I'm your superior. Would you like some tea?"

Remo grunted a no.

Smith continued to gaze into the darkness. "You should know most of your business by now. You have access to the weapons. You'll pick up drop points and communication lines from a clerk in 307 of this building. Of course you'll destroy written matter. Clothing with California labels will be in 102. You'll have money. Identification is for Remo Cabell. Of course, you know the first-name necessity in case of a sudden call."

Smith spoke as though he were reading a list of names.

"We have you as a free-lance writer from Los Angeles. That's optional. You can change that. Method, of course, is your own. You've been trained. We'd like to give you more time, but . . ."

Remo waited by the desk. He didn't expect his first assignment to be like this. But then what did he expect?

The man droned on. "Your assignment calls for a kill. The victim is in East Hudson Hospital in Jersey. He fell from a building today. Probably pushed. You will interrogate and then eliminate him. You won't need drugs for questioning. If he's still alive, he'll talk to you."

"Sir," Remo interrupted. "Where do I meet MacCleary? He's supposed to accompany me on my first assignment."

Smith looked down at the cup. "You'll meet him at the hospital. He's the victim."

Remo's breath slipped out. He stepped back a pace on the soft carpeting. He couldn't answer.

"He's got to be eliminated. He's near death, in pain, and under drugs. Who knows what he'll say?"

Remo forced out the words. "Maybe we can make a snatch?"

"Where would we bring him?"

"Where you brought me."

"Too dangerous. He was carrying identification as a

patient at Folcroft. We've already received word from the police in East Hudson where the fall occurred. There's a direct link to us now. One of the doctors told the police the patient was emotionally disturbed and as far as we know the East Hudson cops have closed it out as an attempted suicide."

Smith swirled the cup. Remo assumed he saw something in the tea. "You will, if he's still alive, question him on a Maxwell. That's your second assignment."

"Who's Maxwell?"

"We don't know. He provides the New York syndicate with what we believe is the perfect murder service. How and where and when we don't know. You will end Maxwell as quickly as possible. If you don't do it in one week, don't look for any more communication from us. We may have to close down and reorganize elsewhere."

"Then what do I do?"

"You can do two things. You can continue after Maxwell. That's optional. Or you can settle down for a while in New York. Read the personals in the New York Times. We'll reach you when we have to through them. We'll sign our messages 'R-X'—for prescription, for CURE."

"And if I succeed?"

The man placed the cup of tea on the desk without turning around. "If you succeed within a week, it'll be business as usual. Take a rest and keep your eyes on the Times. We'll reach you."

"What do I do for money?"

"Take enough with you now. When we contact you again, we'll get more to you." He rattled off a telephone number. "Remember that number. In emergencies—only in emergencies—you can reach me directly on that line between 2:55 and 3:05 each afternoon. At no other time."

"Why are you telling me to hole up if I miss Maxwell?" Remo had to ask the question. Things were moving too fast.

"The last thing we want is you looking up and down channels and then driving into Folcroft one day. So you blow the Maxwell mission. One mission, one training center, it doesn't really matter. But this organization can't be exposed. That's why your first assignment on MacCleary is a must. It's a link to us and we've got to break that link. If you fail in that one . . ." The man's voice tailed off. "If you fail in that one, we'll have to get you. That's our only club. Also you know that if you talk to anybody, we'll get you. I promise that. I'll come myself. MacCleary's in the hospital as Frank Jackson. That's it. Goodbye."

The man turned to shake hands, then apparently thought better of it and folded his arms. "No sense making a friend in this business. By the way, make it a fast job on MacCleary, won't you?" Remo saw the man's eyes were red. He left for Room 307.

CHAPTER SEVENTEEN

The two East Hudson detectives rode quietly up in the Lamonica Towers elevator to the twelfth floor, the penthouse level.

The silence of the elevator's rise seemed to stifle their speech. Detective Sergeant Grover, a round ball of a man, showed the end of a dead cigar and watched the numbers flash by. Detective Reed, "Long Gaunt Reed" as he was known to the homicide squad, ran a pencil along markings in a small black notebook.

"He had to fall from at least the eighth story," Reed said.

Grover grunted assent.

"He wouldn't talk."

"You fall eight stories, you going to talk?" Grover asked. He touched the immaculately polished button panel with a pudgy, hairy finger. "No, he ain't gonna talk. He ain't gonna say nothing. He ain't gonna even make it to the hospital."

"But he was able to talk. I heard him say something to one of the stretcher men," Reed said.

"You heard. You heard. Get off my back, you heard." The blood rushed to the folds of Grover's face. "So you heard; I don't like this whole business. You heard."

"So what d'ya want from me?" Reed yelled. "It's my fault we gotta speak to the owner of Lamonica Towers?"

Grover wiped at a smudge on the polished button panel. They had been a team nearly eight years and both knew the danger of Lamonica Towers.

It was a luxury apartment house fit for the most exclusive sections of New York, yet the builder had chosen East Hudson. He had brought the town $4.5 million worth of taxable real estate, twelve stories high. Lamonica Towers balanced the municipal budget and lowered the taxes of the townspeople. It was a political asset that had kept one party in power for nearly a decade. It rose, white and splendid, among the gray three-story dwellings that huddled at its base.

And the mayor had issued strict instructions to the police force:

—A prowl car was to circle the towers twenty-four hours a day. No policeman was to enter without the permission of the mayor himself. Any emergency call was to receive top priority.

—And if Mr. Norman Felton, the owner, who lived in the 23-room penthouse should call headquarters, the East Hudson Police Department was to be at his service—after the department had first notified the mayor, who might be able to do something personally for Mr. Felton, whose political contributions were generous.

Grover rubbed a coat sleeve across the panel and stepped back to survey his shining. The smudge was off.

"You should've reached the mayor," Reed said as the elevator doors opened.

"I should've. I should've. He wasn't home. Whaddya want?"

A red flush rose to the surface of Grover's puffy cheeks. He gave the panel a last inspection, then left the elevator and stepped onto the deep pile of a dark green foyer carpet. When the elevator doors closed, he suddenly realized there was no button to call it back.

He nudged Reed. They could only go forward to the single white door ahead of them with a large metallic eye in the center. The door was ridgeless and without handles.

The well-lit foyer was like a windowless gas chamber except they couldn't even spy a hole for a pill to drop through into the acid.

The foyer bothered Reed least of all. "We didn't even reach the chief," he grumbled.

"Will you shut up?" Grover asked. "Huh? Just shut up?"

"We're gonna be busted sure as you're born."

Grover grabbed a handful of Reed's wide blue labels and whispered fiercely: "We have to do it. There's a body downstairs. I know these rich people. Don't worry. We'll be okay. There's nothing the chief can do. We got the law behind us. It's okay."

Reed shook his head as Grover knocked on the white door. The rap was muffled, like flesh coming against solid steel. Grover removed his hat and nudged Reed to do the same. Reed fumbled with his black notebook but managed to hold on to his fedora. Grover chomped on the butt of the cigar.

The door opened quickly but quietly, sliding to the left, revealing a black-frocked butler, tall and imposing.

They were sorry for disturbing Mr. Felton, Grover told the butler, but they must see him. A man was found on the sidewalk in front of Lamonica Towers. There was reason to believe he fell from one of the apartments.

Grover and Reed suffered under the butler's stare for a moment. Then he said: "Please step inside."

He ushered them into a large room the size of a banquet hall. The detectives didn't even notice the door quietly slide closed behind them. They gaped at the rich white drapes partially shielding a fifty-foot long picture window. A dark, richly upholstered couch ran the length of a side wall. The room was illuminated by indirect white lighting that seemed like a diffused spotlight for an art exhibit. Modern paintings, each in a different striking setting, surrounded the room like sentinel reminders that two high school graduates had entered a different world from East Hudson.

A black Steinway dominated the far corner of the room. The chairs were works of sculpture, flowing in marble simplicity into lines that blended with the room's decor. Through the picture window, the men could see the red reflection of the setting sun glinting off the sides of passenger ships tied up in New York harbor.

Grover let out a low, long whistle and suddenly

wished he had waited to reach the chief. The cigar in his mouth felt like an indictment against his rearing. He stuffed it, wet and sticky end first, into the pocket of his overcoat.

Reed just kept mashing his notebook into his hat.

Finally, the butler returned.

"Mr. Felton will see you gentlemen. If you'll follow me, no smoking please."

When the butler opened the door to the study, Grover knew he had made a mistake. This was not the East Hudson kind of person he was used to dealing with, not the mayor whom he had known as a shyster lawyer or the leading town physician who while drunk had once fumbled away the life of an infant.

It was a different breed of man who sat in the cherrywood chair, his legs crossed under a cashmere robe, a thin volume on his lap. His graying hair, immaculately groomed, seemed to highlight a strong-lined, somber face. His eyes were light blue and unmoving.

An aura of greatness and elegance seemed to permeate his being, as if his presence lent dignity to the book-lined walls. He seemed like what men should be, but never were.

"Mr. Felton," the butler said, "the two police gentlemen."

Mr. Felton nodded and the butler ushered them into the study. The servant placed two chairs near Felton's knees. To his right was a high-polished oak desk. Behind him, drawn curtains.

Mr. Felton nodded. The butler left. Grover sat down hesitantly. Reed followed.

"We're sorry to bother you," Grover said.

Mr. Felton raised a hand in a gesture of reassurance.

Grover shifted in his seat. His pants suddenly felt hot and wrinkled tight. "I don't know how to begin this, Mr. Felton."

The gray-haired man leaned forward and smiled benevolently. "Go ahead," he said softly.

Grover glanced at Reed's pad and nodded.

"A man was found about an hour ago in front of this building. From the way his body was crushed, we think he fell from one of these apartments."

"Someone saw him fall, you mean," Felton asked in a tone suggesting more of a statement than a question.

Grover tilted his head like a man suddenly seeing a door open where none had been before. "No, no," he said. "No one saw him fall. But we've seen a lot of these plungers and I'm almost sure, begging your pardon, that he came from this building."

"I'm not almost sure," the dignified owner said.

Reed demolished his notebook in his twisting hands. Grover swallowed again, his throat suddenly as dry as a summer sidewalk. He started to say something, but a motion from Felton's hands cut him off.

"I'm not almost sure, I'm positive," Felton said.

The two detectives sat motionless. Felton continued: "There have been several families in this building who have entertained rather . . . how can I say it . . . rather odd types. We have a careful screening process before leasing an apartment, but as you men know, you cannot always be sure of the caliber of tenant. I believe the man jumped or . . ." Felton lowered his head as if gaining strength to force the words out. He looked into the blinking eyes of Grover and said: "God forgive me, I believe he may have been pushed."

Felton stared at the thin volume of poetry on his lap. "I know how horrendous this may sound to you, the taking of a human life. But it is possible, you know. There are cases of it."

If their jobs had not been at stake, Grover and Reed would have been hysterical with laughter at someone telling two homicide detectives that murder actually existed in the world. But what could you expect from someone so refined, who was born with a silver spoon in his mouth and who insulated himself against the world with books of poetry?

Felton went on. "I was on the balcony of my apartment an hour ago, leaning over and looking down at the street below when I saw the man fall. He came off the balcony of the eighth floor. My butler and I went down there, but it is an empty apartment. It has been vacant for some time. No one was there. If the man was pushed, his assailant had escaped. I was going to volunteer this information, but I was so unnerved I had to return here for a few minutes to regain my composure. What a terrible thing."

"Yeah. We know how rough it must be on you, sir," Grover said.

"Rough," Reed agreed.

"Terrible and frightening," Felton continued. "And to think that whoever pushed this person . . . if he was pushed . . . may be living in this very building now."

Felton looked into the eyes of the two detectives. "I'm afraid I'm going to have to ask you a great favor. I've already told Bill and he's agreed."

"Bill?" Grover asked.

"Yes. Mayor Dalton. Bill Dalton."

"Oh, yes," Grover said. "Sure."

"That man who was in the street. The dead one."

"He's not dead," Grover said.

"Oh."

"He will be in a little while, but he ain't yet. Pretty bad though, you know, sir."

"Oh, how terrible. But this may help us. I want you to find out who he is, where he is from, as soon as possible. Before midnight if possible. We have extremely good references and background on all the people living here. If there is some connection, we might be able to find it."

The detectives nodded. "We already started a routine check," Grover said.

"Make it more than routine and I'll see you will be well rewarded."

Grover pushed out his fat, thick hands as though shoving away a second helping of strawberry shortcake. "Oh, no. We don't want nothing like that. We're just happy to . . ."

Grover didn't get a chance to finish his refusal. Felton had smoothly taken two envelopes from the

83

pages of the volume of poetry. "My card is in here, gentlemen," he said. "Please call as soon as you learn something."

When the butler returned after ushering out the two policemen, he said: "You could have bluffed your way through. You didn't have to buy them off."

"I didn't buy them off, stupid," Felton said, flipping the poetry on the desk. He rose from the chair and rubbed his hands.

The butler shrugged. "What'd I say, boss? What'd I say?"

"Nothing, Jimmy. I'm kind of griped."

"What's to worry?"

Felton shot a cold glance at Jimmy. Then he turned his back on him and walked toward the curtains shielding the balcony. "Where'd he come from?"

"What?"

"Nothing, Jimmy. Fix me a drink."

"Right, boss. And one for me."

"Yeah, sure. One for you."

Felton parted the curtains and walked out into the twilight air, twelve stories over East Hudson, on the building he had created.

He brushed some spilled earth from a toppled potted palm with his white velvet slipper. It made a scratching noise against the white tiles of the balcony. He walked to the edge, rested his hands on the aluminum railing and inhaled the fresh air blowing off the Hudson.

The air was clean up there. And he had paid for every brick to get him that high into the cool refreshing breezes. It was free of soot, not like the streets across the river on the lower East Side with pushing crowds, vendors, factories and mothers screaming at kids—when mothers were home. Felton's had rarely been.

Of course, there had been the nights. He would feel a tap on his shoulder, look up, and see his mother and smell the stench of alcohol. There was always a man behind, outlined by the light of the hallway. There was no place else for him to stand. It was a small apartment. One room. One bed. He was in it.

She'd nudge and he'd go out in the hallway. "Hey, leave the pillow," she would yell. And he'd leave it and go outside into the hallway and curl up near the door. During the winter he would bring his coat.

He lived on the top floor then, too. But on Delancey Street on the lower East Side, the top floor was the bottom of the social ladder, even without a whore for a mother. There were no elevators on the lower East Side. The top meant walking.

Sometimes she would lock the door. And then he couldn't sneak into the apartment in the morning to get a jacket or brush his teeth or comb his hair. He would go to school with the hairy dust of the hallway floor still on his back. But none of the students would laugh.

One had tried it once. Norman Felton had settled it in an alley with a broken bottle. The boy had been bigger, by a full half foot, but size never bothered Norman. Everyone had weak points and on the big ones, it was bigger. All the more space for a stick, a rock, a broken bottle.

By the time he was fourteen, Norman Felton had done two stretches in the reformatory. He was headed for his third when one of his mother's sleeping partners left a wallet in his pants. Norman, heading for the sink, picked up the wallet and left the room. It wasn't the first time he had lifted a wallet near his mother's bed, but it was the first time it had been so full. Two hundred dollars.

This was too much to split with mom, so Norman Felton walked down the stairs of the tenement house for the last time. He was on his own.

His success was not immediate. He ran through the two hundred dollars in two weeks. No firms would hire a fourteen-year-old boy, not even when he said he was seventeen. He tried to work his way in with a bookie, but even they wouldn't touch kids as runners.

He had spent his last nickel on a hot dog and was nibbling around it, saving it, caressing it, as he strolled down Fifth Avenue, scared for the first time he could remember, when a large man leaving a mansion bumped into him and knocked Norman's last food to the pavement.

Without thinking, he flailed into the grownup. Before he got off his second punch, two giants were upon him, beating him.

When he recovered consciousness, he was in a large kitchen with servants buzzing around. A middle-aged woman, attractive and heavily-jeweled, was wiping his forehead.

"You certainly know who to take on, kid," she said. Norman blinked.

"That was quite a show out in front of my house." He looked around. There were more pretty women than he had ever seen in his life.

"What do you think, girls?" the middle-aged woman asked. "Does he know who to take on?" The girls laughed.

The woman said "Kid, you're not going to tell anyone about this, right?"

"Got no one to tell," Norman said.

The woman shook her head, smiling with mistrust. "No one?"

"Got no one," Felton repeated.

"Where do you live?"

"Around."

"Around where?"

"Where I can find a place to live."

"I don't believe you, kid," the woman said and wiped his forehead again.

And thus, Norman Felton began his career in the most fashionable house in New York. He made a good errand boy for the Missus and the girls like him. He kept his mouth shut and he was smart.

Later, he found out who had bumped his hot dog, out in the street. It was Alphonso Degenerato, head of the Bronx rackets.

CHAPTER EIGHTEEN

"They all want you, Mr. Morroco," Norman would say. This always insured a five the next time. Morroco would laugh. "You know it too, kid."

Then Norman would lead Morroco up to either Norma or Carol's room. He would return downstairs knowing what the girls would be doing.

The first thing was to get Morroco aroused. That could take twenty or thirty minutes. His potency was all in his mind. Then, with great effort, the girl could end it. Her groaning would be real. Only it wasn't excitement, it was exertion.

Then came the lavish praise, telling Morroco what a wonderful man he was. This, the Missus explained, was what he paid for. And that's how they made fifty dollars a night from Vito Morroco.

He was in the rackets, the girls said. But he wasn't a torpedo. No money in it. All he did was deliver money from one place to another and keep his mouth shut. He was a bag man. And he never lost a penny and he never said a word about his business.

He worked for Alphonso Degenerato who had the Bronx rackets. Sometimes he would carry, so the girls said, one hundred thousand dollars.

Norman would run the errands for the house and keep his eyes open. He watched people. He watched Morroco. He saw the admiral from Washington who paid a girl to dance around him nude and sprinkle powder over him.

He saw the minister who asked to be whipped. He saw the men who needed two women and those who couldn't perform with a dozen. He saw the lonely and the frightened.

And he ran his errands. Pick up a case of hooch here, a woman there; deliver both. Make sure Daisy had her powder. Never call Mr. Johnson by name. Mr. Feldstein appreciated a little bow upon greeting.

The Missus took a liking to him. "Men are run by their balls, their bellies and their fears," she would tell Norman. "First, they're afraid. Then, they're hungry. When both those feelings are gone, they go for what I give them."

Norman listened. But she was wrong. He learned that quickly.

Men are run by their egos; stronger than life, than food, than sex, is pride. A man is without this pride only when it is beaten from him. Left alone, human beings are servants of their pride before their bodies. All else flowed from pride.

He saw it in Johnson, in Feldstein and in Morroco. He saw it in the shiny buttons of the admiral. Men were weak and they were prideful and they lied to themselves. And that was their weakness. It was the Missus' weakness, too. He proved it.

Norman Felton was seventeen and had been at the Missus' for three years when she asked: "Have you had any women?"

"Yeah."

"Which one of the girls?"

"None of them. I get mine outside."

"Why?"

"Your girls are dirty. Like swimming in a sewer."

The Missus laughed. She rolled back her head and shrieked a harsh laugh that sent her weakly leaning against one of the lamps in the kitchen where they were talking.

But when she saw Norman was not embarrassed or cowed, she stopped laughing and began to yell. "Get the hell out of here. Get out of here, you rat scum. I picked you up out of the gutter, you rat scum. Get out of here."

The cook backed away toward her stove. One of the girls ran into the kitchen and stopped in horror. The Missus, for the first time anyone could remember, was crying.

And chuckling softly before her was Norman, the errand boy.

So he had won, but he had no job, no education and little money. What had he won?

Norman Felton walked out into the rain-chilled afternoon with forty-five dollars in his pocket and a plan. A man had to survive. If he could not, he would die. One life lost. His life was as valuable as the next. More so. It was his.

So Vito Morroco, who had never lost a delivery in his life, a good man with a gun and with the muscle, that night coming out of the Missus' place, met the former errand boy.

He met him in a passageway leading from the side exit to the street. Nobody could see who entered or left.

Norman Felton stood in the passageway. "Gee, Mr. Morroco," he said. "I'm glad I seen you. I'm desperate."

"I heard you been canned, kid," Morroco said. The word "desperate" put him on the balls of his feet. Norman suddenly realized how big Vito was. The hand never left the pocket. The cold brown eyes seemed to cut through Norman's will. The scar-creased lip moved into a sneer.

"What do you want, kid? A fin?"

The air in the chill passageway seemed choking stale. Norman felt the metal strip in his own pocket. It was so damned small. He noticed Vito's eyes move toward his pocket. It was now or never.

"No, Mr. Morroco. I need more."

"Oh," Morroco said. There was a bulge in his pocket, too.

"Yeah. I got a plan how we can both make a fortune."

"We, kid? We? Why you?"

"It's like this. I seen a lot of guys come into the Missus' place. But never none like you, Mr. Morroco. I mean, I know maybe a hundred broads who want it real bad but there ain't a guy, a real guy who can give it to 'em. And I heard the broads in the Missus' say they'd be willing to pay you if you didn't pay them."

Vito suddenly smiled. His cold brown eyes warmed.

His hand started to ease from his pocket.

"Yeah, Mr. Morroco," Norman said. "The Missus only lets the girls who have been doing good work have you. That's why I used to have to take you to special ones each time. The ones who deserve you."

"Yeah?" Vito seemed unable to believe it.

"Yeah, and I was figuring, if I could like set you up with women and get maybe twenty per cent."

Vito was chuckling. The scar made a comical criss-cross across his lip. The gold-capped teeth shone under the pale light of the corridor. His hand was out of his pocket, near his forehead, tipping back his hat.

"No crap," Vito said. "You're a smart kid and I like you but I got other . . ." Vito Morroco, thirty-seven, chief bagman for the syndicate, never finished the sentence. He couldn't. A sharp metal blade was in his throat.

The blood flowed and Vito gagged, rolling over the corridor floor, smearing red splotches on the gray concrete. Norman feverishly tried to get to the wallet, look for a money belt, rifle the pockets. Vito rolled and kicked. Dying, he was almost too much for young Norman Felton.

With a jump, Norman landed both feet on Vito's reddened chest as it rolled topside again. A spurting gush of air and blood came out of Morroco's mouth and he was helpless.

Norman had gotten three thousand dollars for that first killing.

That had been the last time he took his money from the victim. More times than he could count, he had been paid by someone else.

And with the money, he bought the clothes and the house and the manners of respectability. He married a respectable woman, with good breeding, and after five years of marriage that produced a daughter, he found that breeding was only clothes deep. When Mrs. Felton was nude, she was just like any other slut going to bed with another man.

And Felton killed without payment. Without a cent.

90

And that had been the first time.

Felton stepped back from the railing and inhaled the fresh Hudson air again. Today, he had killed once more without profit, this time to stay alive.

Where the hell were these men coming from? In the last year, he had been forced to dispose of one snooper in the regular way upon contract, but today the man had gotten so close, so damned effectively close, that only with a lucky break were Felton and two henchmen able to fling him over the railing down to the street right smack into a police investigation.

Felton's breathing came hard. He no longer noticed the purity of the air. Blue veins bulged in his forehead and he clenched his fists.

Someone was after him and it was no amateur. They had claimed one of his best men.

"No amateur," he mumbled and then his thoughts were interrupted when Jimmy, the butler-bodyguard, came out on the terrace with a scotch and water.

"Tony Bonelli's inside."

"By himself, Jimmy?"

"Yeah, boss, by himself. I think he's scared."

Felton glanced down at the light amber liquid in his glass. "Viaselli send him?"

"Right. Mr. Big himself."

"Are you thinking what I'm thinking, boss?"

"I don't know," Felton said. "I don't know." He turned and walked into the den, carrying half a glass of his drink.

A thin, greasy-haired man with hollow cheeks sat on the edge of a chair near the desk. He wore a blue pin-striped suit, a yellowish tie. He twisted a handkerchief in his hands. He perspired profusely despite the air conditioning.

Felton walked to the chair and stood over Tony, who was almost writhing in his seat.

"What's up, what's up?" Tony said quickly. "Mr. Big sent me over here. He said you wanted to talk about something."

"Not to you, Tony. To him," Felton said and slowly

91

poured the rest of his drink over Tony's black shiny hair.

As Tony tried to mop his head with the handkerchief, Felton slapped him hard, once, across the face.

"Now, let's talk," Felton said, and motioned Jimmy to place a chair beneath him.

CHAPTER NINETEEN

The receptionist at East Hudson Hospital unconsciously straightened, pushing forward her chest, when she saw that beautiful specimen come toward her desk.

He walked like no man she had ever seen, with the grace of a dancer yet the sure, strong movements of an athlete. Every motion seemed to flourish in a calm masculine discipline she just knew could create miracles on a mattress.

He wore a well-cut gray, three-button suit, with a white shirt and a brown tie that matched the deep fascination of his eyes. She didn't know if she was smiling too widely as he allowed his strong hands to settle on her desk.

"Hello. I'm Donald McCann," he said.

"Is there anything I can do for you?" she asked. His tailor was magnificent.

"Yes, there is. I'm an insurance adjuster and frankly I'm in a bind."

He seemed to know she would do anything for him; those beautiful eyes just knew it.

"Oh," she said. The supervisor wouldn't be around until 6:30 a.m. She had a half-hour. What was happening to her? What did this man have?

"Yes," he said leaning forward. "I'm responsible for the insurance on a building. And I hear someone fell from it."

She nodded. "Oh yes, Jackson. He's in Room 411, emergency."

"Could I get to see him?"

"I'm afraid not. You'll have to wait until visiting hours and then get permission from the guard. He tried to commit suicide. They don't want him to do it."

The man seemed disappointed. "Well, I guess I'll just have to wait until visiting hours." He waited as though expecting something. Maybe he would leave. She didn't want him to leave.

"Is it very important?" she asked.

He was a kiss away from her lips now. "Yes."

"Maybe I can get the guard down here and you could go in for a minute." To hell with the supervisor.

He was smiling so beautifully. "Would that be all right?" she asked.

"Beautiful," he said.

"I'll phone him. You get in one of those elevators and hold the door open so he'll have to use the other one to come down. The night nurse takes her break now. I'll keep the guard here until I go off . . . about twenty minutes. Then I'll phone to the floor and you hold an elevator there. When the other one comes up, come back down here to me. I'm getting off then. But don't tell a soul. Promise?"

"I promise." He had such beautiful eyes. It wasn't until he had disappeared into the elevator that the receptionist realized her husband would still be in bed when she got home. She'd work out something later.

Remo pressed the fourth floor button and watched the elevator doors close. So Chiun had been right. Some women could sense a man's control of his body. They could be attracted by what he called the *hia chu* charm, knowing within that the man had such perfect timing and rhythm and highly developed senses that he could arouse them every time.

"Man can love. Women live. They are like cattle that feed the body. Their main concern is their safety, nourishment, and happiness. The devotedness that passes for love in the man's mind is really the woman's instinct for protection. She wins that protection by simulating love. She, not the man, is responsible for the life of the human race. A most wise choice."

But how had Chiun been so certain? He had never called for women himself at Folcroft. But he had said: "In your mind, she will respond."

Remo had not intended to use Chiun's method. But then, nothing had turned out the way he expected since

94

the meeting with Smith, that tea-drinking filing cabinet back at Folcroft.

How could CURE with all that superior personnel be so stupid about the special unit's methods. Of course, they were not supposed to know much, but the ignorance he had faced in just getting out was beyond reason.

First they had wanted to load him up with a bulky revolver. Then the armament man displayed a raft of pipe pistols, pen darts, poison dropping rings, all stuff from Charlie Chan movies.

He had been taught how these devices worked in order to know what he might have to face. But carrying around an arsenal was like wearing an advertisement. He had said no and the armament clerk shrugged. If he were to enlist an unwitting ally, then he would call for a drop of one of these instruments. But for himself, Remo knew, his hands could do all the work necessary without having complications from the local bulls.

He had kept the Remo Cabell identification and asked for an increase of only one thing: money. His allotment had been $3,000. He asked for $7,500 and got it. One thousand in small bills and the rest in hundreds.

This was wrong, too much for an assignment, he had been told. It would just draw attention to himself. But then they believed he'd be operating with CURE for the rest of his life.

"Take just what you need." Well, if he were that obsessed with remaining unnoticed, he never would have used the receptionist. He would have come in through the hospital's emergency room and looked as if he belonged there. That was another thing Folcroft had taught him. Remo smiled as he thought of the course in just looking as though you belong, the way to ask questions, the manner, the gait of the walk. Yet, they had kept saying, "Master this and you can forget most of the rest we teach."

Well, he could forget most of what they taught. He wasn't going to find himself in a death cell again for doing his job, or waiting like MacCleary for one of his own to dispatch him. Remo had had it. The world had taught him and he had almost gotten killed before he learned. Not again . . . not ever again.

He would call for a drop of cash in two days, saying he was on Maxwell's tail, then hit a drop with a note that he couldn't even get close, and then for the rest of his life follow the last order from the organization: "Disappear."

But first MacCleary. With MacCleary out of the way, no one would bother him again. The elevator door opened slowly, almost silently.

The hall was quiet in the pre-dawn darkness. A table lamp burned at the vacant desk of the night nurse. Remo walked down the hall. He glided silently on crepe soles . . . 407, 409, 411 . . . no guard. Without breaking stride, he entered the room. He had already made an eyecheck of the hall. But if someone should have been in a shadow, his even stride and quick entry might have confused them as to the room he entered.

He pressed the door closed behind him. He had decided MacCleary would probably have a broken rib from the fall. All he had to do was press one into the heart and no one would think of murder. The room was dark but for a pin light above MacCleary's head. The light reflected off a metal object on the bed. It was the hook. The room smelled of ether. As he moved closer he saw tubes stretching down to the dark form like lines of thick spaghetti.

One leg was in traction. He moved a hand along the warm wettish cast until he felt the plaster around the rib cage. He didn't want to crack it. That would leave signs. He'd have to adjust it, carefully, carefully, the rib cage pivots and . . .

"Hey, buddy," came the faint voice. It was MacCleary. "That's a hell of a way to make an identification. You didn't even check the face."

"Shut up," Remo said.

"I've got a lead on Maxwell."

"Yeah, sure. Sure. Just a minute."

"Okay. You want to finish me without getting the lead, it's your business. But I think you're going to crack the plaster. Bad evidence."

Why didn't he shut up? Why didn't he shut up? How could he kill him while he was talking and knew what was going on? Remo's hands carefully left the plaster intact. He had to put them back. He had to do it.

"I've got a better way," MacCleary said.

"Shut up," Remo said.

"C'mere," MacCleary said.

Remo glanced at the hook arm. It was free. The other was in a cast. So MacCleary was going to bring the hook from behind when Remo leaned forward. Good. Let him. Then he'd just smash him in the throat, rip out a couple of tubes and to hell with the whole mess. He'd be free.

"Okay," Remo said. He leaned forward, balancing to catch the hook from behind with the sweep of his right hand.

MacCleary's face was fully bandaged, too. Only his lips showed.

"I couldn't penetrate," MacCleary said. "But I did get to a man named Norman Felton. He owns the apartment they pitched me out of yesterday. That's Felton with an F like Frank. He's Maxwell's middleman. The syndicate knows him but a lot of them think he's the eliminator. Only the real top guys must know about Maxwell. No wonder we've never been able to get a line on him."

The hook remained still. Remo concentrated on it out of the corner of his eye.

"I saw Felton for just a minute. It was his penthouse I was thrown out of. This damned hook caught on a couch and he was on me with a couple of goons before I knew it. I got one of them, I think."

Remo saw the hook rise. He was ready for it but it just fell back down.

"The goons came out of the walls. Watch the walls, they're inhabited. They all slide every which way. Before they came out, I had Felton backed to the

97

garden windows that lead to his terrace. He was scared, but not enough to talk. Call for drugs at a drop, I don't think he'll break with pain.

"Felton's pretty classy. He's a millionaire by now and he uses that as a cover. I don't even think the local bulls know he's in the rackets. He's got only one interest. That's his daughter, Cynthia. She's at Briarcliff, this fancy college in Pennsylvania. Doubt that she knows what Daddy does for a living. I don't know how you could use her but that's a weakness of his. Maybe you could use her to break him."

The hook moved slightly, but only slightly. Then it was still.

"I guess I screwed up pretty badly. I knew we never should have gone after Maxwell. Not enough facts. That's fatal in our business. But we were stuck with the job. Now you've got to end him. I don't know how, but try something I haven't. I tried to go directly toward him and I'm just another victim.

"Good luck, Remo. Have somebody say a mass for me."

Remo turned and started to walk away.

"Where are you going?" MacCleary hissed. "You've got to finish something."

"No," Remo said.

"For God's sake, Remo, you've got to. I can't move. I'm drugged. They took my pills. I can't do it myself. Remo. You had the right idea. Just pressure the rib cage. Remo. Remo!"

But the door slowly closed on Room 411 in East Hudson Hospital and it was quiet except for the scratching of a hook on a cast.

CHAPTER TWENTY

Remo had been in the bar for hours. The receptionist had muttered something about her husband, finished her drink and left. He was the only one drinking. The bartender just refilled his glass whenever he nodded. A mess of bills soaked up the spilled liquid. The bar was dark and slightly overheated. It was too big and too empty.

Occasionally, the bartender complained about how business had left when the burlesque nearby closed down. It was a tourist bar that had had to go local and couldn't make the switch. Prices were still eighty cents a shot. The bartender never bought one back, as was the custom in New Jersey.

The hospital was about ten blocks away. It was the wrong place to stay, as he had been taught, and it was the wrong thing to be doing. But he was there and he was drinking and he would keep on drinking until he bought a bottle and brought it to a hotel room where he wouldn't be rolled for the cash.

Remo nodded and the glass filled up with a double shot of imported Canadian whiskey. He wouldn't even register at the hotel. He would keep on drinking until he could not think, until he could not feel or know and then he would be rolled undoubtedly and then thrown in jail and then CURE would find him and they would end it all.

They would do a good swift job, as fast as an electric chair, maybe faster. And then the judge's sentence would be carried out and may the Lord have mercy on his soul. Remo nodded again and the glass filled again and some more bills disappeared again and by the white lighted clock over the bar it was one p.m. or something or was it one a.m. or something?

There was sun in the street out there, too much sun

and light. People played in the light, didn't they? They were the day people. And the whiskey was good. It was doing its job. "Whiskey," Remo mumbled, "can contain without taste traces, small amounts of cyanide, any amount of arsenic and various toxic chemicals."

"What, sir?" the bartender asked.

"Toxic chemicals," Remo said.

The bartender, whose greasy graying hair gave him the appearance of an Italian count gone broke, said: "No, this is good stuff. We don't lace it. You're drinking the best."

Remo raised the glass. "To the best. To Chiun."

"To what, sir?"

"Take the money."

"All of it?"

"No. Just for the drink."

The bartender made a sloppy snatch on the extra bill. He'd never pass a CURE test.

"What, sir?"

"Another."

"You haven't finished that."

"I will. Come back. Come back. Come back. Come back." Maybe he should kill the bartender, then he'd be safe in jail. Maybe life. Life. Life. But jail walls didn't stop CURE. Oh, no. Not the team. Protect the team. The team must be safe at all times.

"You played on a team, sir?"

"I played on the best." Damned stool. Remo grabbed the bar ledge. "No one ever got through the center of the line. I lost three teeth but no one ever got through the center of the line. Ha, ha. Until now. I open the gate for them all." Oh, Remo, you're so brilliant. You're so smart. I never knew you were so smart. "They're all going through now."

"Yeah," said the bartender, making an even sloppier snatch. "They're all going through now." He had an evil Italian face. It wasn't a Scotch, Irish, Indian, German or who knew what else face, like Remo's beautiful face. It was ugly. Ugly as Remo's face.

Italians: the image of a people addicted to crime is an improper one and should not be accepted by CURE members. Italian-Americans have one of the lowest crime rates per capita in the United States. The existence of organized crime and its heavy participation by those of Italian descent distorts the picture. There is a cultural trait, however—a mistrust of authority—which appeared during the 1940's. This was brought over mainly by the Sicilians, a people often occupied by foreign powers. The image of the Italian criminal has been enhanced by news coverage of the fewer-than-three hundred, who participate in the upper echelons of organized crime.

In other words, they got caught. Remo remembered the lecture almost in toto. He remembered too much. The glass filled again.

"Just a minute," he said, grabbing the bartender's hand. "That was poorly done." He slapped the hand and three wet bills dropped to the puddle.

"You made the mistake of keeping the area wet so the bills stick together. Keep it dry. Dry is the secret. You have greater manipulation with the dry object. Here watch this."

Remo took a few dry tens from his pocket. He made a fast snatch that marvelled the bartender, then quickly stuffed the bills in the bartender's shirt pocket. "See. Dry."

The bartender grinned with an embarrassed smile and shrugged with his palms turned upward. An Italian gesture.

Remo slapped his face. The crack echoed through the empty bar. The man stumbled back against a shelf of bottles. They jingled but didn't fall. He clasped his left hand to his right cheek.

"Never try such a sloppy job on me again," Remo said. The man waited a few moments, breathing hard and staring at Remo who smiled and nodded. Then the bartender checked the bills in his pocket and found they were gone. The customer's hands had just moved

101

too quickly. Even drunk, the speed had been blinding.

"Muscles. I'm training your muscles. Want to try again?" Remo offered the dry bills, but the bartender just backed away.

"I oughta call the cops," the bartender whined, moving toward a part of the counter that Remo judged held the bar stick.

"By all means, do that," Remo said. "But first another double, my clumsy man of the untrained muscles."

"One double coming up," the bartender said as he moved back to Remo. He kept close to the bar with his left hand beneath it, an advertisement of a weapon. By the time he reached Remo, his pace and balance telegraphed that he would bring some sort of stick up in an arc over the counter toward Remo's head.

The bartender stopped, the stick came in a sweep. As fast as it moved downward, Remo's hand moved upward. His hand smashed against the middle of the stick, stopping it, but acting as a pivot against which the top of the stick kept moving. The stick cracked and the bartender quickly yanked his swinging hand to his chest. The vibration had stung.

Remo nodded for another drink and from then on he was not disturbed. Maybe he could tour the country, doing tricks. Then CURE would be more hesitant about killing him.

Hell with it. He was sentenced to die by a judge and he was going to die. A good thought occurred to Remo. He let himself down from the stool and went to the men's room. When he got out, he slumped into a booth and motioned the bartender who brought his drink and all his money. There wasn't a cent missing. Remo gave the man a ten spot.

At first, the bartender refused to accept it, but then slowly, cautiously, conceded to Remo's whim. "For your honesty," Remo insisted. Then he began his serious drinking.

He came to at the same table. Someone was shaking his shoulder. The bartender was yelling, "Don't touch that guy. He's murder," and the shaking continued.

Remo looked up. The bar was darker. His head felt as if it were closing in a vise, his stomach existed only by the pains in it. And he was going to puke. And the shaking stopped.

Remo glanced up, briefly up, mumbled thanks and stumbled to the bathroom where he dry-heaved for an eternity until he saw an open window. Standing on his tip toes, he sucked the fresh air into his lungs in a rapid pace, then faster and deeper until his body was consuming twice the amount of oxygen a running man consumes. Into the base of the groin, hold, out full, the whole essence of your being out, into the base of the groin, hold, out full, the whole essence . . .

His head still ached when he normalized his breathing. Remo splashed some water on his face, combed his hair, and rubbed the back of his neck. He would walk in the fresh air for an hour or so and then eat, something like . . . like rice.

The bartender and the man who had shaken him awake were talking as he picked up his money from the table.

"You recover pretty fast, Johnny," the young man said, shaking his head. "I thought you'd crawl out."

Remo forced a smile. He said to the bartender: "Anything I owe you?"

The bartender backed away, his hands raising slightly in a defensive position. He shook his head. "No, nothing. Everything's fine. Fine."

Remo nodded. The bartender seemed too scared to have checked his papers. They had been in order and the thin strip of tape on his wallet had not been disturbed, when he checked his cash.

"I hear you're full of tricks," the young man said. "*Karate*?"

Remo shrugged. "Ka-what?"

The young man smiled. "From what I heard, you were doing *karate* tricks in here this morning."

Remo glanced outside. It was dark. The light from a newspaper office's sign shone into the street. He must never reveal himself like that again. He'd be remembered at the bar, maybe for a long time.

"No, I don't know anything like that." He nodded to the young man and the relieved bartender. "Well, good night," he said and headed toward the door.

He heard the bartender mumble something about his being "a wild one," and the young man answered: "Wild? What about the guy who cut his own throat at the hospital this morning? Only one arm and that one with a hook on it and he still cuts his own throat. I mean if a man wants to kill himself . . ." Remo kept on walking.

CHAPTER TWENTY-ONE

The local newspaper had it in detail. "Man Kills Self on Second Try; Jump Fails, Hook Works." They didn't leave out anything.

The man, a mental patient from a New York sanitarium which thought him sufficiently cured for outpatient treatment, had jumped yesterday from a twelve-story building on Avenue East, police said.

They said he was guarded round the clock with no one allowed in the room. "Miraculous," said doctors about the way he allegedly ripped open his own throat with the hook that replaced an amputated hand.

"It's amazing he could do that" a hospital spokesman said. "He was in traction and it must have taken tremendous effort for him to get that much pressure behind the hook. Where there's a will, there's a way," the spokesman alleged.

Detectives Grover and Reed said flatly, "It was suicide."

Meanwhile, another suicide victim was recovering in the Jersey City Medical Center. Mildred Roncasi, 34, of 1862 Manuel Street . . .

Remo dropped the damned paper in a trash can. Then he hailed a cab. That nut, MacCleary. That idiot. That fool. That damned fool.

"What's holding you up now?" Remo asked the driver. The cabbie leaned over the back seat. "Red light" he said.

"Oh," Remo answered. And he was quiet as the cab let him off at St. Paul's Church, where he completed an errand, then hailed another cab that took him to New York.

Remo didn't sleep that night. He didn't rest in the

morning. He just wandered until he reached the telephone booth at 232nd Street and Broadway in the Bronx. A stiff, chill, autumn wind blew across Van Cortland Park. Children played in the drying grass. The sun was orange and setting. It was three p.m. He stepped into the telephone booth and shut out the wind. A group of Negro boys were scrimmaging in motley uniforms. They banged away at each other and piled on. Remo's attention rested on a small boy with no helmet but his kinky hair. Blood ran from beneath his left eye. An apparent knee injury forced him to hobble when he jogged to the line from the defensive huddle.

He saw one of the big backs on the opposing team yell something and point to the boy. The boy yelled back and waved his arms in an obscene gesture. The quarterback handed the ball to the big back who followed his interference into the center of the line. Miraculously, the offense stopped, right at the small boy's slot. When the pileup peeled off, there was the little boy with no helmet, a big cut and a bigger grin. An idiot grin by a dumb black kid who didn't know enough to get out of the way. CURE should've gotten that kid. He and MacCleary. Go, team, go.

Remo slowly dialed the special number. Between five to three and five after, he had been told, it would ring on a local line in Folcroft. Smith would pick up with a 7-4-4 code signal.

Remo heard the buzzing and casually watched the little Negro return another challenge with another obscene gesture. Again the plunge. Again the pileup. And the boy got up with a tooth missing, but the grin was there.

Pretty soon, no more teeth. Remo wanted to yell out: "Kid, you stupid kid. All you'll get is brass teeth and a broken head."

"7-4-4," Smith's voice interrupted Remo's thoughts.

"Oh. Hello, sir. Williams. I mean 9-1."

The voice was steady. "That was a good job at the hospital. All ends sewed up. Very neat."

"You really liked that, didn't you?"

106

"Yes and no. I would rather it had been me. I knew the man . . . but that's beside the point. We only have three minutes. Anything?"

The plunge was on once more this time with the big buck in the new uniform and shiny helmet driving straight at the kid, who didn't blanch. He crashed toward him, but the squirt ducked under to hip height, rammed his feet behind him and drove. Beautiful tackle.

"Anything?" Smith repeated.

The kid slapped his knee and tried to make light of his hobble back to the huddle. But this time it was an offensive huddle. He had held. The little dumb kid, bloody-faced, with no helmet, nothing but a strand of guts somewhere, had held. No one had passed. They weren't able to move over his hole.

They couldn't break him and somewhere there was something worthwhile and if the whole damned world and its rotten judges and slimy politicians, its crooks and emperors had tried to go through that slot, they would have hit a wall that wasn't going to move for anybody. Not an inch. And that was worth something even if nothing else was. Not for the rest of his life would that kid forget that he had done something and no matter what curves the world threw at him, he would have that.

And MacCleary had had it. He had had it in spades. And if he wasn't there now, he didn't have to be. Because MacCleary had held. And that little nigger kid had held. And that's what it was all about, this whole rotten stinking world.

And Chiun was wrong. Vietnam was wrong. You didn't let someone crash your home and if you died at the doorstep, then you were dead. But you had stood there and no one passed and it didn't matter a sneeze in a windstorm if no one wrote it down or paid you. You had done it. You. You were alive. You lived, you died, and that was it.

"Anything? Any lead?" Smith's voice was loud. "We'll be cut off soon."

107

"Yeah. I have a lead. You'll have Maxwell's head in a bucket within five days."

"What? You sound violent."

"You heard what I said. You'll have his head or mine."

"I don't want yours. Be careful. That was an excessive amount of money you took. Frankly, I didn't expect . . ."

The line went dead.

Remo left the telephone booth. The kid was sitting on the sidelines, holding his head.

"Hurt?" Remo asked.

"No, just a little."

"Then why's it bleeding?"

"Ah got hit."

"Why don't you wear a helmet?"

"Helmet?" the boy laughed. "They cost money."

Remo reached into his pocket and handed the kid a twenty dollar bill. "You're a dumb bastard," Remo said, and then he walked away. He needed a shave.

CHAPTER TWENTY-TWO

Felton knew that fear had a point of diminishing returns. The shaking Italian before him could be no more terrorized than he was at that moment, trembling in the chair of Felton's study.

From here on in, more threats would only diminish fear and action could somehow strangely eliminate it. He had seen too many people afraid of beatings until the first blow, afraid to die until they saw the finger tighten on the trigger.

"We're going to hold you awhile," Felton said.

Bonelli groaned. "Why me? Why me?"

"Simple. You're Carmine Viaselli's brother-in-law. You people are strong for family."

Bonelli slid from the chair to his knees. "But nobody comes back when you have 'em. Please, on my mother's grave, please."

Jimmy, the butler, standing behind Tony's vacated chair, chuckled. Felton shot him a dirty look. The smile disappeared, but Jimmy's large, raw-boned hands began to rub together like a man anticipating a meal.

"You'll be safe," Felton said, leaning back in his leather chair, raising a leg over the other so that his kneecap was nose level with his guest. "As long as I'm safe, you'll be safe."

"But I came free. Nobody brought me. Why all of a sudden, after twenty years, this? Why?"

Felton uncrossed his legs quickly and leaned forward. Veins bulged in his massive neck. He looked down at Bonelli's slick combed head and yelled: "Because you don't give me the answers!"

"Whadya want to know? If I know, I'll tell you. Honest. I swear on my mother's grave." He pulled a silver medal from beneath his shirt and kissed it. "I swear."

"All right. Who is coming after me and why? Why the pressure? Who'd gain but your brother-in-law?"

"Maybe some other syndicate?"

"Which one? Everything's settled. You tell me, Tony. You tell me everything ain't decided over a conference table or in some damned guinea kitchen. You tell me, huh? You gonna tell me?"

Tony shrugged, a supplicant in a temple whose god knew only wrath.

"Tell me it's the cops, Tony, tell me. Tell me about one-armed cops that come in killing. Tell me about 'em. Tell me about an Internal Revenue man poking around my junkyard in Jersey City, tell me what he's doing. Or bartenders who get people interested into moving into Lamonica Towers. Tell me it's cops when a hooked torpedo says he wanted to rent in the Towers and then goes for my throat. Tell it to me, Tony."

Beads of sweat formed on Felton's forehead. He rose from the chair. "Tell me."

"Carmine didn't send 'em. I swear."

Felton swung his body around and leaned over yelling. His hands flailed the air. "You didn't send 'em?"

"No."

"I know you didn't send them."

Bonelli's mouth opened. He gaped unbelieving.

"I know you didn't send them," Felton yelled again. "That's what's bothering me. Who? Who?"

"Please, Felty, I don't know."

With a sweep of his hand, Felton dismissed his guest. "Jimmy, get him to the shop. He's not to be hurt. Yet."

"No. Please. Not the shop, not the shop. Please." Tony ripped the medal from his neck, imploring for mercy. Jimmy's large hands grabbed the padded, pin-striped shoulders and lifted the guest to his feet.

"Get him out of here," Felton said like a man asking that lobster shells finally be removed from his plate. "Get him out of here."

"Right, boss," Jimmy laughed. "C'mon, Tony baby, we're gonna take a trip. Yeah. Yeah."

When the sliding door clicked shut, Felton walked to the cabinet bar and poured himself a massive shot of Scotch in a tumbler. His castle had been breached. The Tower had holes. And for the first time, Norman Felton was not attacking.

He swilled down the drink, made the face of a man unaccustomed to heavy drinking, poured another, looked at it, then returned the liquid-filled glass to the cabinet. Well, now he would attack. He didn't know where, but he knew as all jungle animals do that there is a time to kill or be killed, there is a time when waiting means only counting the minutes to death.

He walked out on the balcony again and watched the lights on the George Washington Bridge that linked the two great eastern states.

He had ruled as champion in these states for nearly twenty years. And in a decade, he had never had to use his own muscles until . . . he glanced at the broken palm pot . . . until tonight.

He had built up a system of contract torpedoes and sub-let torpedoes. With just four regulars who could buy the hit-men and with the perfect way to get rid of bodies, he reigned unmolested in the quiet of Lamonica Towers.

But one of his regulars, O'Hara, had bought it, right in the living room. One blow, a slash of the hook, a head opened and twenty-five percent right off the top, the top of the system.

Felton stared at his hands. Now there were three: Scotty in Philadelphia, Jimmy here, Moesher in New York. A multi-million-dollar system and it was under attack from an invisible enemy. Who? Who?

Felton's hand tightened into a fist. There'd have to be hiring. Moesher would lay low and come in only on cue. Jimmy would stay in the Towers.

It would be like the forties again when nothing could stop him, nothing, not the crummy rotten world, the cops, the FBI, the syndicate, nothing could stop him. When, with his hands and mind, his team had made Viaselli, the punk, chief in the east; made a second-rate

111

numbers banker the king and kept him there.

Felton breathed deep the clear cool night air and a smile formed on his face for the first time that night. The tinkling of a phone floated out to the patio.

Felton returned to his study and picked up the black receiver on the mahogany desk. "Yes?"

"Hi, Norm," came the voice, "This is Bill."

"Oh, hello, Mayor."

"Look Norm, I'm just calling about that suicide. He carried identification as an outpatient from Folcroft Sanitarium. It's in Rye, New York. Ever hear of it?"

"Oh, he was mentally disturbed."

"Yes. Looks like it. I spoke personally to the director up there, a Dr. Smith. And, Norm, I warned him that if he released any patients who are cuckoo, he's responsible. By the way, Grover and Reed were all right, weren't they? I have them here right now. They gave me the lead on this Folcroft."

"They were fine," Felton said. "Just fine, Bill."

"Right. Anything I can do for you, just buzz."

"I'll do that, Bill, and we'll have to have dinner some night too."

"Right, bye."

Felton waited for the click, then dialed.

A voice at the end said "Marvin Moesher's residence."

"This is Norman Felton. Please put Mr. Moesher on the line."

"Certainly, Mr. Felton."

He hummed as he waited in his study.

"Hello, Marv. *Vas masta yid?*"

"Eh," came the voice from the end. "Nothing . . . and you?"

"We got troubles."

"We've always got troubles."

"You know where Scotty is?"

"Home in Philly."

"We may have to do some hiring again."

"What? Just a minute. Let me close the door. This is an extension phone, also. Just to be safe."

112

There was a moment of silence. Then Moesher again: "Business picking up?"

"Yes."

"I thought we had cleared the market."

"A new market."

"Viaselli expanding?"

"No," Felton said.

"Someone expanding?"

"I don't think so."

"What does O'Hara say?"

"He passed away this morning."

"Mine gut."

"We won't be doing any hiring yet. There's some things we have to find out."

"Speak to Mr. Viaselli?"

"Not yet. He sent a representative for preliminary talks."

"And?"

"And he's still talking."

"Then it might be Mr. Viaselli who's . . . ?"

"I don't think so. I'm not sure."

"Norm."

"Yes."

"Let's retire. I got a nice house in Great Neck, a wife, a family. Enough's enough. You know. Why tempt fate?"

"I've been paying you good the last twenty years?"

"Yes."

"You do much work in the last ten?"

"You know it's been nothing."

"Jimmy, Scotty, and O'Hara been carrying your load?"

"Scotty ain't been working either."

"He's going to now."

"Norm, I'm going to ask a favor. Let me retire?"

"No."

"All right." Moesher's voice was resigned. "How we going to work it?"

"First, ground work. There's a place called F-O-L-C-R-O-F-T. Folcroft. It's a sanitarium in Rye."

"Yes?"

"Find out what it is. Try to rent a room."

"Okay, Norm. I'll get back to you."

"Marv? I wouldn't be calling if I didn't need you."

"Forget it, Norm. I owe this much. I'll give you a buzz tomorrow."

"Love to the family."

"Zama gazunt."

Felton replaced the receiver and clapped his hands. A private sanitarium. No government office to hide behind. That was it.

He made two more phone calls that night. One to Angelo Scottichio in Philadelphia; and the second to Carmine Viaselli.

CHAPTER TWENTY-THREE

The Paoli local clacked along on its ancient tracks through the Pennsylvania countryside. Remo Williams gazed out of the dusty window at the Philadelphia suburbs, inch for inch some of the most exclusive property in America.

This was the fashionable Main Line country surrounding the ghetto that Philadelphia had become. Here the aristocrats of the nation retreated for the final stand against the poor. They had surrendered Philadelphia to the common man a generation ago.

It was a dull, wet afternoon, a chill gray reminder that man should be holed up in his cave around a warm fire. It reminded Remo of his school days, his chore as class monitor, center of the line in high school, and failure after two years of college.

He had never liked school. Maybe it was the schools he went to. And now he was going to see the finest women's school in the Country: Briarcliff, without the publicity of Vassar or Radcliffe or the innovations of Bennington. A gaggle of brainy broads and he was going to have to convince one of them to bring him home to Daddy.

Remo lit a cigarette when he saw others ignoring the no-smoking sign. He was careful not to inhale the smoke into his breathing pattern.

Chiun had been right. Put enough pressure on him and he'd revert. It was the same old story. Remo puffed again. The houses, most of them two-story brick, had personality, lawns, and just breathed old money. Homes.

MacCleary's words came back to him. "No home, no family, no involvements. And you'll always be looking over your shoulder."

The cigarette was good. Remo toyed with the ash

and reviewed his mistakes. He never should have remained in the area after the visit to MacCleary, never should have played games with the bartender, never should have approached that hospital receptionist. A white jacket in almost any hospital would have given him anonymity and passage into any room. It was done, though. That was it. Over. Probably nothing fatal.

Now all he had to do was kill Maxwell, whoever the hell he was. Felton was the key, but his sanctuary seemed unapproachable. Felton's daughter would be his passport. He undoubtedly kept his daughter totally ignorant of Maxwell's organization. He wouldn't have sent her to Briarcliff College if he didn't. She probably had no idea of what Felton did for a living, MacCleary had said.

Briarcliff. She must have brains, real brains. What would he talk to her about? What would be her interests? Nuclear physics, social democracy versus an authoritarian state, Flaubert, his failings and future in the new art form of the novel?

He was just Remo Williams, ex-cop, ex-Marine, and full-time assassin. Would he compare the efficacy of the garotte to the speed of a knife, discuss the elbow as a killing instrument, the windpipe's vulnerabilities, lock-picking, movements? How was he going to open a conversation with a Briarcliff girl? This wasn't any receptionist or waitress.

Remo's thoughts were suddenly interrupted. Someone was staring at him. It was a girl to his left. Her eyes dropped back to the book when he looked up. Remo smiled. Even the most brilliant had their erotic zones. A woman is a woman is a woman. The conductor bawled out: "Briarcliff. The town and the school. Briarcliff."

CHAPTER TWENTY-FOUR

Felton dressed slowly in his master bedroom. He snapped the garters onto his black socks. He slipped on his dark blue trousers, then pulled tight the laces on his black shining cordovans. He turned to look at the full length mirror. His chest, encased in an undershirt, expanded full. Not bad for a man of fifty-five.

He stared at his thick neck and solid arms, linked by massive shoulders. He could still bend a ten penny nail in his fingers, still crush a brick in his hands.

Jimmy moved silently into the room, carrying before him, in his large hands, a mahogany box. Felton noticed him in the mirror, standing behind him, a good eight inches taller than himself.

"Did I tell you to bring the box?"

Jimmy smiled broadly. "No."

"Then why did you bring it?" Felton turned to catch a side profile of himself. He flexed his arms. His triceps swelled large and powerful. He forced his right hand against his left and extended them before him. The view in the mirror was a magnificent display of tanned, rippling muscles.

"Why did you bring the box?"

"Thought you'd need it."

Felton threw his arms behind him and cocked his head as if glancing at an oncoming bull, the matador Felton, supreme, victorious.

"Need?"

Jimmy shrugged. "It's convenient, boss."

Felton laughed, laughed with teeth that never had a cavity, showing gums that never gave him a day's trouble in his life.

"Now!" Felton yelled. "Now!"

Jimmy backed away, flipping the highly-shined mahogany box on the bed. "It's been ten years, boss. Ten years."

"Now," Felton said, grabbing his last look in the mirror. "Now."

Jimmy coiled his large frame like a spring. Felton held his right hand behind his back and waved his left in front of him, fingers wide and palms outstretched. He sneaked another look at the mirror and Jimmy sprang.

Felton caught the thrust by throwing his left shoulder, arm straight, into the charge. No finesse. No leverage. Just sheer power.

Jimmy's large Texas frame seemed about to envelop the smaller man but at the height of his rush, Jimmy let out a grunt and stopped moving forward.

Felton's large hand was in his chest. It would not be budged. Felton gave a flick of his wrist. Jimmy flailed his arms and yelled as his body bounced backward.

Like a jungle cat, Felton moved forward, grabbing Jimmy's arms, preventing him from crashing his back into the floor. He roared: "Still got it?"

"You still got it, boss. You still got it. You should've gone into pro football."

"I leave that for you Texans, Jimmy," Felton said with a loud laugh, pulling Jimmy's arm with a yank that brought the raw-boned man to his feet.

Jimmy shook his head to clear the cobwebs. "We're ready, boss?"

"We're ready. Bring me the box." Felton purposely refused to look at the wooden container until he had buttoned a white shirt, put on a black knit tie and gone to his desk and removed a shoulder holster of gray suede-like leather from a drawer.

Then he nodded for the box to be opened. Jimmy carefully lifted the lid. Three gun-metal blue revolvers rested on white suede.

"O'Hara won't be needing his," Jimmy said. "Can I take two?"

"No," Felton said. "Is O'Hara's body at the garage?"

"Yeah. Under wraps. Same guys watching it who're looking after Tony."

"When we get back tonight, we'll get rid of O'Hara and his revolver, and let Tony go."

"Wouldn't ita been easier, boss, just to report O'Hara as killed? I mean it's going to feel funny getting rid of him like that."

"And let the locals know my chauffeur got his skull crushed? I don't want this apartment pinpointed as that hooked guy's last stand. No, we have to get rid of our own."

Felton strapped the shoulder holster on. Jimmy shrugged and removed from an envelope in the lid of the box, six official cards in laminated plastic. They were gun permits. One for New Jersey, one for New York, two each for three men, one of whom wouldn't need his again. Jimmy put the permits on the bedspread. They lay there like penny-pitching cards, old photographs of their owners in the corner.

Jimmy—a sharp, drawn face. Felton—smooth with wavy hair, the bright blueness of his eyes shining even in the black-and-white postage stamp picture. O'Hara—a wide, grinning face that now had a puncture in the skull.

They were special permits, made out to financier and industrialist Norman Felton, and bodyguards James Roberts and Timothy O'Hara.

They were special because the pistols were special. Each permit meant that the ballistics test of the pistol was registered in Washington. A bullet fired through the barrel of each gun carried ballistics markings of the barrel that identified its source as surely as fingerprints.

The only time bullets had gone through the barrels on the three pistols were when the ballistics tests were made.

Felton lifted his pistol and Jimmy released a spring switch that slid open a secret drawer in the bottom of the box. There were seven more pistol barrels and a small Allen wrench.

They each put new barrels on their pistols, barrels

whose ballistics markings were known only to corpses.

Felton mused aloud. "Jimmy . . . Moesher was never meant for this business like you and me. He'd have us all living off what we make in the junk-yards." Jimmy just grinned. Felton playfully punched Jimmy's shoulder and Jimmy pretended to block it. They were both grinning.

"No sir," Jimmy said, wrenching tight the barrel of his revolver. "You gotta love your work."

"I don't love it, Jimmy, but it's necessary. It's something natural, very natural, that some of us do." Felton thought a moment, then said: "It's natural and necessary. This is a jungle, Jimmy. Nobody ever gave us anything."

"Nobody gave us nothing, boss."

"The world made us what we are. You know I could have been a doctor, a lawyer, even a scientist."

"You would have been the greatest," Jimmy said.

"I would have been good."

"Everything you do, boss, is good. Honest."

Felton shrugged. "It has to be. Who'll do it for us?" He bounded over to the long closet near the full-length mirror and slid two closet doors in opposite directions.

The closet extending the full sailboat length of the room held a row of suits that for quantity might put a Robert Hall's to shame. In quality, it was Saville Row.

Felton kept thumbing through the blue suits looking for the jacket that matched his pants. The only way he could tell was by finding one without pants. After eight suits, he said to hell with it, and took the jacket.

"Jimmy?"

"Yeah, boss."

"You're a good man."

"Thanks, boss. What brought that on?"

"Nothing. I just wanted to say it."

"You ain't afraid something's going to go wrong with Viaselli?"

"No. Not Viaselli."

"That hooked guy?"

Felton buttoned the blue jacket that matched
120

perfectly with his pants, except he knew it didn't belong with those pants.

Jimmy knew better than to press the point. When Felton was ready to talk, he would talk and not before. Jimmy put the revolver inside his jacket pocket.

Later that night, Felton was in a talking mood. Jimmy was at the wheel of the pearl gray Rolls Royce Silver Dawn, subbing for O'Hara. He drove over the George Washington Bridge, its high-wired lights glinting like an Italian festival, its span stretching onward to New York like a great aqueduct of ancient Rome, except it carried people, not water.

"You know," Felton said, staring at New York from the back seat. "I was sorry I missed World War Two."

"We had a war of our own, boss."

"Yeah, but World War Two was a war, a big one. It's a hell of a thing that somebody's gotta go to an engineering school on the Hudson to learn how to run a war."

"You could've done it better, boss."

Felton frowned. "Maybe not better on the war side, but I would've known enough to look out for the Russians."

"Didn't we know?"

"We knew, but I would've known better. I would've looked out for England, France, China, the works. That's what the game is, Jimmy. Outside the family, you got no friends. There's no such thing as friends. Only relatives."

"You're the only family I ever had, boss."

"Thank you, Jimmy," Felton said.

"I mean it. I'd die for you or Miss Cynthia."

"I know it, Jimmy. You remember how that hooked guy came on?"

"Yeah, boss. I was right behind him."

"Ever see a guy move like that before?"

"You mean at you?"

"No. No, not that so much. Just the way he moved. He came without telegraphing that he was coming on."

"So?"

121

"Do fighters telegraph punches?"

"Not good ones."

"Why not?"

"They're taught," Jimmy suggested.

"That's right."

"So?"

"So, who's teaching?"

"Guys can learn it lots of places," Jimmy said. Felton was silent for a few moments.

He asked, "Seem more difficult lately to make a hit?"

"Yeah, kinda."

"Is it the fault of the help? They getting worse?"

"About the same. You know, young punks, got a gun, they'll foul it up if you don't lead them by the nose."

"But what was their big trouble?"

"They said their targets were getting tougher to hit."

"But what else?"

"I don't know. Nothing else."

"No. There's something else."

Jimmy turned onto the West Side Drive heading for downtown New York. He eased the car into the right-hand lane. It was a Felton order. When on a job, obey the misdemeanors. No littering, no loitering, no speeding or double parking. It had always worked well.

"There's something else, Jimmy."

"You got me, boss."

"First they were hard to hit. And second, they never hit back. None of those mugs we hired ever got shot or even hurt."

Jimmy shrugged his shoulders and looked for the 42nd Street exit. The conversation was beyond him. The boss was working on another one of his ideas.

"Why weren't any of these guys armed?" Felton asked.

"Lots of people don't carry guns," Jimmy said as he turned into a ramp that led down from the elevated highway.

"People checking into Viaselli's operations or mine?"

"So they're stupid."

"Stupid? No, they've got a pattern. Patterns and stupidity don't mesh. But that guy with a hook was a change from the pattern. If we thought that hooked bastard was fast, watch out for what comes next. I feel it. I know it."

"You mean they're going to get better."

"I don't think we're going to see much better. I don't think there is better. But watch out for teams. Killer teams."

"Like we had in the forties?"

"Like we had in the forties." Felton leaned back in his seat.

CHAPTER TWENTY-FIVE

The doorman at the Royal Plaza on 59th Street near Central Park was surprised when the well-dressed occupant of the Rolls Royce insisted the doorman park his car so that his chauffeur could accompany him.

The doorman agreed quickly. One does not argue with Rolls Royce passengers.

Felton made sure Jimmy was behind him before they both entered the plush Plaza lobby, with its heavy gilt-crested chairs, ponderous plants and effeminate room clerk.

The gun and shoulder holster fit neatly beneath the suit, and Felton and his driver attracted little attention as they stepped onto the elevator.

"Fourteenth floor," Felton said.

Jimmy slipped his right hand into his black uniform pocket to adjust his weapon. Felton gave him a quick dirty look that told him the move was wrong.

The gold-tinted elevator screen doors opened into a small foyer. Every other floor opened to a hallway with rooms. But Felton had advised Viaselli when he rented the floor in the Royal Plaza to reconstruct the entrance, eliminating the hallway in favor of a box-like entrance with peepholes.

Felton waited in the foyer and winked at Jimmy who smiled back. They both knew the arrangement of the floor and knew that one of Viaselli's body guards right now was looking them over through a one-way mirror on their left. Felton adjusted his tie in the mirror and Jimmy made an obscene sign toward his reflection with a middle finger.

The door opened. A man in a dark pin-striped suit and a bluish silk tie invited them in.

They walked calmly like a team of dancers, never showing emotion or quickening their pace, into a large, well-lit overfurnished living room filled with clouds of gray smoke and enough men in business suits to start a convention.

Only it wasn't a convention. And when Felton and Jimmy stopped in the middle of the room under a gaudy chandelier, the talk suddenly stopped and the whispering began.

"It's him," came the whispers. "Heah, that's him. Yeah. Shh. Not so loud, he'll hear you."

A well-manicured little man with a black knotted Italian cigar stuck between his thin dark lips came over to Felton and Jimmy, waving a thin bony right hand and flashing a twisted smile.

"Eh? *Come sta*, Mr. Felton?"

Felton tried in vain to remember the man's name. He smiled a guarded recognition.

"Can I get you something to drink?"

"Thank you, no."

The man clapped one of his hands over his chest as if restraining a bleeding heart from bursting outward onto the gold yellow carpet. "I hate to mention this, but him"—the man said bowing slightly toward Jimmy, "this ain't no place for drivers. There's gonna be a meeting, you know."

"I didn't know," Felton said, looking at his watch.

"He gotta go."

"He stays."

The little man's expressive hands opened palm outward, his shoulders hunched. "But he don't belong."

"He stays," Felton said without expression.

The smile that never had been a smile disappeared as the thin dark lips tightened over yellow teeth. The right hand cupped toward its owner's face in a familiar Latin gesture. "Mr. Big's going to have something to say about this."

Felton glanced at his watch again.

The little man retreated to a cluster of compatriots

125

grouped around a sofa. They listened to him, casting sidelong glances at Felton and his chauffeur.

Jimmy busied himself by staring down everyone in that group.

Suddenly, there was a rustle in the room as everyone seated jumped to their feet and those standing unconsciously straightened their backs. They all looked toward the big double doors that had been flung open.

A man in a conservative gray suit and striped Princeton tie stood in a doorway and called out: "Mr. Felton."

Felton and Jimmy walked across the living room to the doors, feeling all the stares of the men behind them. Jimmy stopped at the doors while Felton entered. Jimmy waited like a sentry and then, with his cold gray-blue Tennessee eyes, took on the whole room.

The double doors had always fascinated Felton. Facing the living room, they were gold-encrusted and ornate. But on the other side, they were fine, old, oiled wood, fit for any executive's office.

The air was different too. You could breathe without inhaling smoke from a dozen cigars. The floor had no carpeting and it creaked as Felton walked over to the end of a long mahogany table at the end of which sat a finely-groomed gentleman staring at a chess board.

He had deep, friendly, brown eyes set in a firm, noble Roman face. His hands were manicured, but not polished. His hair was long, graying at the temples, but combed conservatively with a part at the left side.

He had woman's lips, full and sensuous, yet there was nothing effeminate about him. Behind him, on the wall were pictures of a stately matron and eight children, his family.

He did not look up from the chess board, as Felton sat down in a chair at his elbow.

Felton inspected the face for aging, the hands for a tremble, the body movements for hesitancy. There were none. Viaselli was still a potent man.

"What move would you make, Norman?" Viaselli asked. His voice was even, his pronunciation Oxford excellent.

"I don't know chess, Carmine."

"Let me explain it to you. I am under attack by the black queen and the black bishop. I can destroy the queen. I can destroy the bishop." Viaselli's lips closed and there was silence.

Felton crossed his legs and stared at the figures on the checkered board. They meant nothing to him. He knew Viaselli wanted a comment. He would not give it.

"Norman, why should I not destroy the queen and the bishop?"

"If I understood chess, Carmine, I would tell you."

"You would be a worthy opponent if you learned the game."

"I have other games."

"Life is not the limit of your endeavor, Norman, but the extent of it."

"Life is what I make it."

"You should have been an Italian."

"You should have been a Jew."

"It's the next best thing." A warm smile crossed Viaselli's face as he pondered the board. "What I never could understand was your fondness for Southerners."

"What fondness?"

"Jimmy from Texas."

"Merely an employee."

"Merely? It never appeared like that to me."

"Appearances are deceiving."

"Appearances are all there is."

"I have your brother-in-law," Felton said, anxious to end the philosophy.

"Tony?"

"Yes."

"Ah, that brings back the problem of the black queen and the black bishop. Should I destroy them?"

"Yes," Felton said, "but not when you're out-numbered."

"Outnumbered?"

"Just you, me and your man. You're outnumbered," Felton said nodding to the conservatively dressed gentleman at the door.

127

"And all my people in the living room?"

"An evening's entertainment for Jimmy."

"I don't think so, but nevertheless, you are not the black queen and black bishop. You are my white queen, the most powerful piece on the board. For you to turn black would be disaster for me, considering that I am under attack."

"I am under attack too."

Viaselli looked up from the board and smiled.

Felton placed a hand on the table. "Who are we fighting?"

"I'm glad you said we, Norman." Viaselli softly clapped his hands. "I'm glad, and yet I don't know. A Senate committee is coming to our area, probably in two weeks. Yet we've been under surveillance now for five years. Does the Senate prepare that far in advance? No, I don't think so. And the investigations have been different. You have noticed. With the FBI and the tax men, investigations would end up in court. But these five years of men snooping around have not ended up in court."

"You mentioned a Senate investigation?"

"Yes. The Senate is working its way east across country and will be here soon. All of a sudden there have been more people snooping around."

"That accounts for the increase in targets in recent months."

"I think so. But there's something else that's strange. You are under attack?"

Felton nodded. "Another family fight among you guineas?"

Viaselli's cheeks reddened, but he showed no other emotion. "No," he said. "We have a new opponent. I do not know who or what he is. Do you?"

"I may know in a couple of days."

"Good. I want to know too. Now you can return Tony."

"Maybe."

Carmine became silent. He had a way of silence that he could use more effectively than words. Felton knew

128

that to reopen the conversation would give Carmine the edge. And all Carmine needed, despite Felton's feeling about how much he did for the man and how much the man needed him, was for Felton to make the first move and he would be lost.

It had been that way twenty years ago, only then Viaselli didn't have his headquarters in the Royal Plaza Hotel.

CHAPTER TWENTY-SIX

It was the back of a grocery store which Viaselli's father ran for a living. Instead of the fancy carved ivory chess pieces, Viaselli was leaning over a wooden case on which were painted black and white squares. He was pondering the cheap wooden pieces when Felton entered.

The summer-hatched flies dominated the room. Viaselli looked up.

"Sit down," he had said. "I want to talk about money."

Felton stood. "What does a second-rate numbers runner know about money?"

Viaselli moved a pawn forward. "I know there's a war on. I know there's a lot to be had. I know you're not getting much of it."

"I'm getting enough."

"Two grand a job on a contract basis? Is that enough for a smart Jewboy?"

"It's more than dumb guineas make."

Viaselli moved a bishop from the opposite side of the board.

"Today, yes. Tomorrow?"

"Alphonso isn't going to let you make any more. Blood or not, he doesn't trust you. I've heard."

"And if Alphonso is dead?"

"Giacomo takes it."

"And if Giacomo is dead?"

"Louis."

"And if Louis is dead?"

Felton shrugged. "It would take a plague to kill that many."

"And if Louis is dead?" Viaselli moved a knight endangering the bishop he had brought out from the other side.

Felton shrugged again. "You bring me here to pass the time of day?"

"And if Louis is dead?" Viaselli repeated.

"Someone else."

"Who else?"

"Whoever has the balls."

"Flaherty. Would Flaherty take over?"

"No, he's not a wop."

"What am I?"

"A wop, but it don't mean you're going to grab the whole works just because your name ends in an 'I'."

Viaselli moved out another knight. "It's a good beginning," he said. He looked up from the board again. "Look, what kind of a Jew are you, working for someone else all the time?"

"You want me to work for you?"

Viaselli moved his queen. It was one move to mate. He recited: "You kill Alphonso. You kill Giacomo. You kill Louis. Then . . ."

"Then what?" Felton said.

"Then who's going to kill you?"

"You."

"With what? You'll be the only one around with artillery. The only one with any brains, anyway. The whole syndicate will be disorganized."

"Then why don't I rub you out, and take over myself," Felton asked.

"Because you're not a wop. Every Mafioso would be gunning for you. They don't trust any but their own. You'd be a danger."

"And you wouldn't?"

"I'm one of their own. They'll learn to live with me. Particularly if I can get things going again."

He looked long and hard at Felton. "What's your future now? Two guineas fight and you wind up dying for the money. A couple of lousy grand. Is that any way for a Jew to die?"

"Dead is dead."

"But you can live. And on top of the pile."

"And you don't doublecross me?"

"You'll be my queen. My most powerful piece. Doublecross my queen?"

"How about your torpedoes?"

"I won't have any."

"The ones you inherit."

"I send them away, Chicago, Frisco, New Orleans. You will be my army. The only way to make this business pay, without trouble, is to separate the money makers from the troublemakers. No one who works for me will carry a gun. You'll do all that work. You get paid, not by the job, but by salary and a percentage of the take. Get rid of Alphonso, Giacomo and Louis, and you'll start off with one million dollars."

"I wish I understood chess."

"You could be a master," Viaselli said.

But Felton didn't have time for chess. From the East Side, he rounded up Moesher, the kid who would stand all day and fire pistols at targets. Angelo Scottichio he found at a bar, planning a cheap heist that would earn him less than one hundred dollars. Timothy O'Hara came off the docks where he specialized in petty larceny of Army equipment. Jimmy Roberts was a cowboy out on his luck, with a big Texas mouth that found him with gun in hand listening to a heavyset young man who had just hired him as a killer.

"You will be my generals," Felton told the four. "As long as we operate like a military machine, we will survive and win and get rich. Real rich."

"We can also get killed," grumbled Moesher.

"Only until we get rid of those who've got the muscle to kill us."

The first hit was Alphonso Degenerato, head of the Bronx rackets who chose to live in an unassailable Long Island mansion. But he was not in his mansion when a hired torpedo named Norman Felton approached him with four other men.

Alphonso was in bed with a chorus girl in her upper East Side apartment overlooking the East River. He knew he was safe because only his nephew, Carmine Viaselli, knew where he was. He would have found the

132

East River quite cold had it not been for the lead sedative administered by the five young men and the warming company of the lovely and quite-dead chorus girl.

Giacomo Gianinni was a quiet man who never toyed with chorines. He was strictly business. On the good recommendation of Carmine Viaselli, the grieving nephew of Alphonso, he met secretly with a torpedo to plan the revenge of Alphonso. He met the young torpedo on a penthouse roof. The torpedo brought four other men with him, all of whom tried desperately to stop Giacomo from jumping off the roof.

And then Felton received a phone call from Viaselli. "They know it's you, Norman," he said.

"Then they're sure as hell going to know it's you, too, booby."

"It's not that bad," Viaselli said. "There's only Louis left. But he expects you. No surprises this time. But one thing. Make the body disappear."

"Why?"

"Then I have bargaining power. My people are susceptible to mysteries."

Louis lived on a yacht and never left it. He had telephone connections and speedboats to carry his orders out and his money in.

To Felton, it was impossible. He was just waiting to be killed, just waiting for Louis to muster the torpedoes to do the job. Then Louis made a mistake. He quietly tied up his yacht on the shores of the Hackensack River in Jersey City, near an auto junkyard.

It was World War II. Junk, steel, metal were in demand. Louis docked his yacht and within fifty-five minutes Felton had paid four times what the yard and its junk-processing machinery was worth. It was every cent he could round up. But what good is money without life?

It was a very simple plan when the former junkyard owner explained how the machine worked. And when Felton saw the machine, he laughed and laughed.

133

"Gentlemen," he told his four generals, "our future is made."

That night, the yacht's hull was ripped open by some kind of missile. The next day, over a bullhorn, Jimmy called to the yacht to see if they wanted the hull repaired.

"We can't leave the vessel," came the answer.

"You don't have to leave. We'll tow you ashore and fix you while you're docked."

After ten minutes, the men on the yacht agreed.

Junk yard cranes were moved into position. Heavy steel cables were fastened to the front and rear of the ship. The cranes began to hoist and tug. They jerked the yacht up a water-slicked mud runway to the top of an incline, which suddenly spilled downhill into a large concrete block house, reinforced with slabs of steel. The yacht and its crew slid into the block house and never came out.

The next day, Felton received another call from Viaselli. "Magnificent. Did I tell you one million dollars? Make it two million dollars. How did you do it? The crew, the yacht and everything."

"I don't waste all my time on chess," Felton answered. The next few years were easy. Moesher, the crack shot, did most of the work, eliminating witnesses against Viaselli. Their bodies vanished.

O'Hara kept recruiting, kept tabs on all the young torpedoes trying to develop within Viaselli's mob. He'd hire them once, then eliminate them. Scottichio built a minor empire in Philadelphia, again under Felton's control.

Jimmy rumbled along following his boss's orders. It was a lot safer than riding brahma bulls. Felton had been able to keep clean. His name came up in no investigations; he kept out of the front line of action; he built a life of respectability.

Only his four men knew anything about Felton's operation. And they would not talk. The mystery kept them all on top of the heap.

It had been a profitable deal for all. And now Felton

stared at Viaselli pondering fancy chess pieces in the Royal Plaza Hotel, and he wondered how long the profits would last.

"You're still my white queen, Norman," Viaselli said, resting his hands on the long mahogany table. "There is no one else."

"That's nice," Felton said, watching Viaselli make the final move to mate. "Then, who is Maxwell?"

Viaselli looked up quizzically. "Maxwell?"

Felton nodded. "Whoever is going for us has something to do with a Maxwell. I killed a man this afternoon whose only interest was this Maxwell."

"Maxwell?" Viaselli stared in puzzlement at the board. Were new pieces entering the game?

"Maxwell?" Felton repeated.

Viaselli shrugged. Felton cocked an eyebrow.

CHAPTER TWENTY-SEVEN

It was easy to get into a room alone with a Briarcliff student, much easier than sneaking into a brothel. Not that Remo had ever sneaked into a brothel. It was just that madames were much shrewder than deans of women. They had to be. They were dealing with more complicated things than the intellectual development of a new generation of women.

Remo merely told the Dean of Women that he was writing an article for a magazine dedicated to the metaphysics of the mind. He wasn't sure what that meant, but the dean, a heavyset, cow-like matron with a strong nose and a hairy chin, agreed to give him the run of the campus until eleven p.m., when, of course, propriety dictated a women's campus should be free of men. At that time, the dean of women said, gently caressing a pencil, Remo could report to her in her quarters and she would help him review the notes for the article.

Thus, Remo found himself in Fayerweather Hall, scribbling notes he would never need on a cheap steno pad he intended to throw away, as a dozen young, obnoxious, loud, enthusiastic young women shouted their opinions on "What is Woman's Relation to the Cosmos?"

They all had opinions. They all crowded the couch on which Remo sat. Hands, smiles, voices assaulted him. And each girl, he asked the same question: "And your name?" And each time, he didn't get the answer he wanted. Finally, he said "Are there any more girls in this dorm?"

They shook their heads. Then one said, "Not unless you count Cinthy."

Remo perked up. "Cinthy? Cinthy who?"

"Cinthy Felton." The girl laughed. "The curve-breaker, the grind."

"That's not nice," said another student.

"Well, it's true," the other said defensively.

"And she's where?" Remo asked.

"In her room, where else?"

"I think her opinion is worth hearing, too. If you'll excuse me, girls. What's her room?"

"Second floor, first right," a chorus responded. "But you can't go up. Rules."

Remo smiled politely. "But I have permission. Thank you."

He mounted the steps, polished with a half-century of shine, rubbed by thousands of feet of wives of presidents and ambassadors, glowing in a dusky half-light from cheap old lamps. You could bottle the tradition surrounding Fayerweather Hall, it was that strong.

It was a smell, a feeling. Traditions? Remo smiled. Someone had to start somewhere, had to start a tradition somehow, and if enough years passed between the original stupidity and its ultimate worthlessness, that, sir, was tradition. Where had he heard that definition of tradition? Had he made it up?

The first door on the right was open. He saw a desk, a light splashing on it, and a rather coarse leg sticking from beneath it. An arm, at the end of which were five stubby nail-bitten fingers, moved from behind the high-shelf portion of the desk which concealed its user.

"Hello," Remo said. "I'm doing a magazine article." It was a hell of an introduction to a woman he would have to convince to take him home to daddy.

"What are you doing here?" Her voice was a composite of adolescent squeak and matron rasp.

"I'm writing an article."

"Oh."

She pushed her chair over so she could see Remo. What she saw was a big, handsome man silhouetted in the doorway. He saw another of the generation of moral crusaders: a girl with a blue skirt and a brown

137

sweater, wearing white tennis shoes. Her face was pleasant, or could have been pleasant if she had worn makeup. But she wore none. Her hair was wildly frizzled, like a wheat field in the wind. She chewed on the point of her pencil. On her sweater was a button, "Freedom Now."

"I'm interviewing students."

"Uh-uh."

"I'd like to interview you."

"Yes."

Remo fidgeted. His feet somehow needed shuffling. He attempted to concentrate on her essence, to project his manhood as Chiun had taught, but somehow his mind was up against something not quite a woman. She had breasts, hips, eyes, mouth, ears, nose, but the essence of woman, womanliness, had somehow been bled out of her.

"May I interview you?"

"Certainly. Sit down on the bed." Coming from any other woman, this might have had the overtones of invitation. Coming from the girl before him, it was a logical suggestion to sit down on the bed because there was only one chair in the room and she was in it.

"What's your name?" Remo asked, displaying the pad.

"Cynthia Felton."

"Age?"

"Twenty."

"Home?"

"East Hudson, New Jersey. A gritty town, but Daddy likes it. Sit down."

"Oh, yes," Remo said, lowering himself to a bluish blanket. "And let's see, what do you think is the woman's relation to the cosmos?"

"Metaphysically?"

"Of course."

"Essentially woman is the child bearer in an anthropoidal society, bounded on one hand by the society per se, that is empirically correct, rather to say . . . are you taking all this down?"

"Of course, of course," Remo said increasing the pace of his scribbling to keep up with the incomprehensible academic imbecilities of his subject. At the end of the interview, he conceded he did not understand all that he had been told, but would like a further explanation of some of the finer points.

Cynthia was sorry, but she had a full day the next day.

The writer pleaded that only she could help unravel this metaphysical knot.

"No," was the answer, "definitely not."

Perhaps then, asked the writer, she would have breakfast with him.

No, was the answer again, she had a full schedule.

Then, perhaps, asked the writer, she would give him a picture of her blue, blue eyes.

Why, was the question, did he want a picture of her blue, blue eyes?

Because, was the answer, they were the bluest, blue eyes the writer had ever seen.

"Nonsense," was the retort.

CHAPTER TWENTY-EIGHT

Cynthia was to have been at the restaurant at 9:15. With any other woman tardiness wouldn't have been unusual. But with these social purpose types, they lived almost like men. Punctual, efficient.

If MacCleary couldn't penetrate, the penthouse must have traps. What the hell would he be getting into?

Remo fingered the glass of water before him. Somehow Vietnam was different. You could always return to your own outfit. At night, you knew someone else was on guard if you weren't. There was protection.

Remo sipped the water that tasted too much of chemicals. There was no protection in this racket. No retreat. No group. For the rest of his life he would always be attacking or retreating. He put down the glass and stared at the door. He could walk out now, just leave the restaurant, and get lost forever.

Remo forced his eyes away from the door. I will read the paper, he told himself. I will read the paper from the first page to the last and when I am done I will leave this restaurant, drive to New Jersey, find Mr. Felton and see what Maxwell's man can do.

Remo read words that meant nothing. He kept losing his place, forgetting which paragraph he had read. Before he finished the lead story, someone snatched the paper from his hands.

"How long does it take you to read a paper?" It was Cynthia, in a blouse, a skirt and a big clean smile, wrinkling the paper as she stood by the table. She dropped the bundled paper on a passing tray, startling the waiter who never got a chance to give her a dirty look because she didn't bother to glance at him for a reaction.

She sat down and plopped two thick volumes on the table.

"I'm famished," she announced.

"Eat," Remo said.

Cynthia tilted her head in mock wonder. "I've never seen anyone so glad to see me. You've got a grin on your face as if I'd just promised you a hundred years of healthy living."

Remo nodded and leaned back in the seat. He flipped her a menu.

The dainty little Briarcliff junior, whose mind was created only for aesthetic pleasures, downed an orange juice, steak and waffles, chocolate sundae, two glasses of milk, and a cup of coffee with two cinnamon buns.

Remo ordered fried rice.

"How quaint," Cynthia exclaimed. "Are you into Zen?"

"No. Just a light eater."

"How fascinating." At the last cinnamon bun, she began to talk. "I think your story should be about sex," she said.

"Why?"

"Because sex is vital. Sex is real. It's honest."

"Oh," Remo said.

"It's what life's about." She leaned forward waving the cinnamon bun like a bomb. "That's why they destroy sex. Give it meanings it was never supposed to have."

"Who are 'they'?"

"The structure. The power structure. All this nonsense about love and sex. Love has nothing to do with sex. Sex has nothing to do with love. Marriage is farce perpetrated on the masses by the power structure."

"Them?"

"Right. They."

She bit viciously into the bun. "They've even gone so far as to say that sex is for reproduction. That, thank God, is dying out now. Sex is sex," she said, spraying crumbs. "It's nothing else." She wiped her mouth. "It's the most fundamental experience a human can participate in, right?"

141

Remo nodded. This was going to be too easy. "And in marriage, it gets most fundamental of all," he said.

"Crap."

"What?"

"Crap," Cynthia said casually. "Marriage is crap."

"Don't you want to get married?"

"What for?"

"For fundamental experience."

"It only clouds the issue."

"But your father. Don't you want to make your father happy?"

"Why didn't you mention my mother?" Cynthia asked, her voice suddenly becoming cold.

Whatever you say, say it fast. Throw her off. Make it wild. Remo shot the words out: "Because I don't believe she exists. If she did, she'd have to be a woman. And there's only one woman in the world. You. I love you." Remo grabbed her hands before she could release nervous energy with them.

It was a risky ploy, but it worked. A flush seized her face, she stared down at the table. "It's rather sudden, isn't it?" She looked around the room as though the world had agents monitoring her love life. "I don't know what to say."

"Say 'Let's go for a walk'!"

Her voice was barely audible. "Let's go for a walk."

Remo released her hands. The walk proved profitable. Cynthia talked. She couldn't stop talking and always the conversation returned to her father, his occupation and his apartment.

"I don't know what he does with the stocks but he certainly makes a lot of money," she said as they passed a jewelry shop on Walnut Street. "You don't care about money, Remo. That's what I like about you."

"But your father's the one who deserves praise. It must be an awful temptation when you've got a lot of money to play playboy."

"Not Daddy. He sits in that apartment. It's as if he's

142

afraid to go out in a cruel and vicious world."

Remo nodded. The air had a faint smell of burned coffee grounds. The chill of late autumn cut through his jacket. The noon sun gave out light but no heat.

Down the block a man stared in another window. He was tall and heavily built. He had passed Remo and Cynthia twice since they had left the hotel.

"Come," Remo said, tugging at Cynthia's hand. "Let's walk this way." Four blocks later, Remo knew Cynthia rarely lived at home, that the walls of the apartment were very smooth, that she never knew her mother, and that dear daddy was just too tender and kind to the servants. Remo also knew they were being tailed.

They walked and talked. They lingered beside trees, they sat on rocks and talked about life and love. When it was dark and unbearably cold, they returned to Remo's room in the hotel.

"What would you like for supper?" Remo asked.

Cynthia toyed with the dials of the television set, then made herself comfortable on a lounge chair. "Steak. Rare. And beer."

"Right," Remo said, picking up the white phone. As he called room service, Cynthia looked about the room which was furnished in Twentieth Century Characterless. Just enough loud colors to break the hospital atmosphere, but not enough to be striking. It was a room designed by a committee for the average man to live in.

Remo mumbled the order to room service and watched Cynthia draw her knees up to her chin. She would have to do something about her scraggly hair.

As soon as Remo put down the phone, it rang almost as if returning the receiver triggered the bell. Remo shrugged and smiled at Cynthia. She smiled back.

"They're probably out of steak," he said. He picked up the receiver. A low voice at the other end said: "Mr. Cabell?"

"Yes," Remo said. He tried to visualize the face that

143

belonged to the telephone voice. It was probably the character who was tailing them. Did Felton keep a guard on his daughter?

"Mr. Cabell. This is very important. Could you come down to the lobby immediately?"

"No," Remo said. He'd see how far this caller would go.

"It's about your money."

"What money?"

"When you paid your bill at the bar yesterday, you apparently dropped $200. This is the manager. I have it in the office."

"I'll settle in the morning."

"I'd rather we settle it now. We don't like to take responsibility."

"The manager, you say?"

Remo knew he was tactically pinned. He was in a room with enemies outside. They knew where to get him. Maybe MacCleary was right about no place to lay your head. In any case, he was no longer attacking with surprise. Two days on the job and he had blown his major advantage.

He noticed his hand was wet on the receiver. He was perspiring. He breathed deeply, drawing oxygen down deep into his abdomen. Well, here he was. Now or never. Number one for CURE. He rubbed the flat of his palm against his trouser leg. An exhilaration came over his body.

"Okay. I'll be right down."

He hung up and went to the closet and took out a suitcase. Folded inside it was the coat he had worn the day before. He moved his hand down the lining of the left sleeve until he felt a long thin metallic object. Carefully blocking Cynthia's view, he removed it and slipped it into a small slit in his belt. Sodium pentathol. If pressure points failed to unlimber speech, this would succeed.

"I'll have to go out for a few minutes," he said. "It's a contact for a story."

"Oh," Cynthia said showing annoyance. "It must be

a wonderful contact. It must be the greatest story of your life to go running out of here like this."

"It is, my dear, it is." Remo kissed her but she backed away angrily. "I'll be right back," he said.

"I may not be here when you come back."

Remo shrugged and opened the door. "That's life."

"Go to hell," she said. "If you're not back when I finish dinner, I'm leaving."

Remo blew her a kiss and shut the door. As it clicked, a blinding flash of light spun through his brain and the green carpeting of the foyer came up to meet him.

CHAPTER TWENTY-NINE

He came to in the back seat of a darkened car. The man who had been tailing him that afternoon sat on his left cradling a revolver in his right hand. He wore a sharp hat well suited for a salesman. It almost shielded a face well suited for a German butcher.

A thin man in front with a homburg was smiling. Then there was the thick neck of the driver. They were obviously parked in the suburbs. Remo noticed trees but no lights from nearby houses.

Remo shook his head, not so much to clear it but to notify his captors he was awake.

"Aha," said the man in the homburg. "Our guest is awake. Mr. Cabell, you don't know how terribly sorry we are that you suffered that accident back in the hotel. But you know how slippery hotel floors are. Feeling better?"

Remo pretended almost total disability.

The man in the homburg went on. "We will not tell you why we brought you here. We will just explain a few facts." He brought a cigarette to his lips. He had no weapon in his right hand.

"We have kidnapped you, Mr. Cabell. We could all go to the electric chair for this, correct?"

Remo blinked.

"And if we were to kill you, we could get no worse punishment. But do we want to kill you?"

Remo was motionless.

"No," the man answered his own question. "We do not wish to kill you. Not necessarily. What we want is to give you $2,000."

The light from the man's cigarette illuminated his smiling face. "Will you take it?"

Remo spoke. "Since you insist and since you've gone to so much trouble, what could I do but accept?"

"Good," said the man under the homburg. "We want you to spend it back in Los Angeles where you came from."

He lifted his left hand—no weapon there, either—and put out the cigarette. "We want you to go back to Los Angeles immediately," he said. His voice was suddenly harsh.

"If you do not, we will kill you. If you mention this to a soul, we will kill you. If you come back, we will kill you. We will watch you a long, long time to see that you keep your bargain. And if you do not, we will kill you. Understand?"

Remo shrugged. He felt the gun jammed into his ribs. He lifted his elbow casually, slightly above it. "That's perfectly clear and fair," he said, "Except for one thing."

"What's that?" said the homburg.

"I'm going to kill all of you." His left elbow came down on the German butcher's wrist and his left palm snatched the pistol. His right hand lashed out at a mark underneath the homburg, between the ear and the eye. His left hand jammed the pistol butt under the butcher's nose and the driver turned to meet a flat chop right at the base of his skull. Some bones snapped. Remo could feel it. Like blocks of wood at Folcroft.

He could hear Chiun chiding. Swift—accurate, accurate, accurate. The mark. Remo carefully knocked out the butcher, then slid into the front seat. He checked the driver slumped to the corner of the wheel. Blood was coming from his mouth. He'd never come to.

He looked to homburg. Maybe his stroke had been off. He felt the man's head, running his finger tips over the temple. He could feel the separated bones, the oozing warm fluid running from the eyes. No luck, dammit, homburg was dead too.

He returned to the back seat where butcher was reaching for space. He grabbed an arm and waited a few moments. Then he twisted the arm behind butcher's back and lifted until the first sound of pain.

147

"Felton," Remo whispered into the cauliflower ear with the tuft of hair growing from it. "Felton. Ever hear of him?"

"O-oh," butcher yelped.

Remo lifted the arm higher. "Yes, yes. Yes."

"Who is he?"

"I never seen him. He's Scotty's boss."

"Who's Scotty?"

"The guy you was talking with. Scottichio."

"With the homburg?"

"Yeah. Yeah. The hat."

"Did Felton tell him to come here?" Remo asked, jerking higher on the arm.

"Jeez. Please. Oooh. Yeah. That's what Scotty said. That Felton told him he was afraid somebody might be trying to bother his daughter. That's the girl you was with. We was supposed to watch out for her."

Up went the arm. "Now for your life. Maxwell."

"What?"

The arm went higher, the shoulder muscles and tendons began to rip. "Maxwell."

"Don't know him. Don't know him. Don't know him. Jeez."

Snap. The arm rose over the butcher's head and he slumped forward. Remo reached into his belt. The needle was bent. The hell with it, Remo thought. He wasn't lying.

Remo looked at his watch. Forty minutes since he'd left the hotel room. He couldn't be far.

He climbed to the front seat, put his arms under homburg's shoulders and with a grunt lifted him over the seat to the rear. Then he did the same with the driver. Moving them was rougher than killing them. He lifted the keys from the ignition, then hopped out of the car. In the trunk of the car, which he noticed for the first time was a dark Cadillac, he found a tarpaulin. He removed it, shut the trunk and returned to the car. He threw it over the two corpses, then folded it back halfway for one more occupant. He pulled the butcher down onto the pile with his fat face sticking up. Then

148

he killed him, covered all three with the tarpaulin and started the car.

He found he was on a side road and quickly discovered the road that led him back to town. He parked the car on a main thoroughfare. The police were lucky that night. None of them stopped him. Remo locked the car and pocketed the keys. Who knew what they would unlock?

CHAPTER THIRTY

"You bastard," Cynthia shouted as Remo opened the door. "You rotten, filthy, bastard."

Her girlish face was red with anger. Her normally scraggly hair showered around her head like a splintered wicker basket.

She stood, her hands jammed on her hips, beside the bed on which was strewn his steak, salad, and potatoes. Her lipstick blotched the mirror over the bureau. She had obviously written several messages, crossed them out as she thought of better ones, then decided to tell him off in person.

"You swine. You left me here and went out drinking."

Remo couldn't control himself. He suppressed a laugh which erupted in a broad grin.

The Briarcliff junior swung her right hand around, palm flat, aiming at Remo's smiling face. Before Remo could stop, his own left hand was up to meet the blow and his right was headed toward her solar plexis straight, flat, his deadly fingertips closing on target.

"No," he yelled desperately, but even yanking back and lowering his thrust, he couldn't stop it. "No," he yelled again, as Cynthia lurched forward into his arms, her eyes rolling back, her mouth open.

She moved her lips as if trying to say something, then slumped to her knees. Remo grabbed under her arms and held on. He started to haul her to the bed, saw the mess there, and lowered her gently to the gray rug floor.

He had missed the ribs and the solar plexis. The blow had only knocked her wind out. Remo knelt down on the carpet and lowered his head to hers. He widened her lips with his thumbs, then slowly breathed into her mouth, while he pressed and released on her stomach.

Cynthia began to squirm. Remo lifted his head and stopped the artificial respiration. Damn his hands. Damn his reflexes.

"Darling, are you all right?" he asked softly.

She opened her eyes, beautiful, blue, searching. She moved her lips again, then breathed deeply. She lifted her arms and enveloped Remo's shoulders. She tilted her head upwards and drew him toward her.

Remo kissed her hard, forcing her head back down to the rug. She found his right hand and rubbed it on her belly, moving it upward to her breasts. As Remo blew gently in her ear, she groaned. Then she whispered, "Darling, I want you to be the first."

Remo was the first. In a tangle of arms, tears and groans, Remo made his entry and exit on the rug.

"I never thought it would be like this," Cynthia said. Her blouse lay behind her head, her bra dangled from the bed and Remo lay on her skirt, cradling her young body in his arms.

"Yes, dear," Remo said. He kissed the running tears on her pink cheeks, first one side, then the other.

"It was terrible," she sobbed.

"There, there," Remo said.

"I never thought it would be like this. You took advantage of me." Cynthia sucked in air over trembling lips on the verge of another tearful breakdown.

"I'm sorry, dear. I just love you so much," Remo said, keeping the timbre of his voice low and reassuring.

"All you ever wanted from me was sex."

"No. I want you. The whole metaphysical, cosmological you."

"Sex. That's all you wanted."

"No. I want to marry you."

"You'll have to," Cynthia said firmly, the flow of tears subsiding.

"I want to."

"Will I get pregnant?"

"Don't you know?" Remo asked incredulously. "I thought you knew so much about this sort of thing."

"No, I don't."

"But the talk at lunch."

"Everyone at school talks like that and now . . ." Her body trembled, the lower lip shook, her eyes closed, tears flowed, and Cynthia Felton, exponent of sex, pure, clean and basic, bawled: "I'm not a virgin anymore."

Until dawn, Remo kept telling her how he loved her. Until dawn, she kept demanding reassurance. Finally as the sun rose and the steak bones on the bed dried a lacquer brown and red, Remo said: "All right. I've had enough."

Cynthia blinked. "I've had it," Remo snarled. "This morning I am getting you an engagement ring. You will get dressed and we will go to New Jersey where I will ask your father for your hand. Tonight. Tonight."

Cynthia shook her head. The wicker basket hair bobbed like the rear springs on a Volkswagen. "No, I can't."

"Why not?"

"I don't have anything to wear." She lowered her head and stared at the rug.

"I thought you didn't care for clothes."

"Not around campus."

"We'll go to any store you like."

The philosophy major pondered a moment as though contemplating the verities of true love, the meaning of it all, then said: "Let's get the ring first."

CHAPTER THIRTY-ONE

"What do you mean, three thousand dollars?" It was Smith's voice, sharp and angry.

Remo rested the phone between his shoulder and chin, as he rubbed his hands for circulation in the cold telephone booth at Pennsylvania Station in New York.

"That's right, three grand. I need it for a ring. I'm in New York. We made a side trip. She insisted on Tiffany's."

"She insisted on Tiffany's?"

"Yes."

"Why does it have to be Tiffany's?"

"Because she wants it that way."

"Three thousand . . ." Smith mused.

"Look," Remo said, trying to keep his voice from carrying outside the booth. "We've spent thousands and haven't penetrated that place yet. With just a crummy ring, I'm going to waltz in and you're bitching over a measly three grand?"

"Three grand isn't measly. Just a second, I want to check something. Tiffany's. Tiffany's. Tiffany's. Hmmmm. Yes, we can."

"What?"

"You'll have a charge account there when you arrive."

"No cash?"

"Do you want to get the ring today?"

"Yes."

"Do it by charge."

"And remember," Smith continued. "You've only got a couple of days left."

"Right," Remo said.

"And another thing. When engagements are broken, girls often give the ring back if they're . . ."

Remo hung up the phone and leaned back against the glass wall. He felt as if someone had drained his intestines.

CHAPTER THIRTY-TWO

It was the first time Remo had ever ridden across the George Washington Bridge in a taxi cab. When he was a youngster in St. Mary's Orphanage in Newark, he had never had the money. When he was a cop, he had never had the desire.

But just twelve minutes before on Fifth Avenue in New York City, he had hailed a cab and said "East Hudson, New Jersey."

The driver refused at first until he had seen the $50 bill. Then he shut up and drove crosstown to the West Side Drive and directly onto the bridge's new lower deck, which wags called the Martha Washington.

Cynthia kept staring at her 2.5 karat square-cut engagement ring, moving her taut long fingers back and forth like a slow, horizontal yo-yo, giving her eyes the reassurance at multiple ranges that she had fulfilled her prime objective in life—she had gotten her man.

Her normally scraggly hair was coiffured into a sweeping crest that rose slightly above her head, framing her finely chiseled features.

A hint of mascara hid her lack of sleep and seemed to give her a seductive maturity. She wore lipstick in a dark enough shade to be modest, yet feminine.

A ruffled blouse set off her long, graceful swan's neck. She wore a sophisticated brown tweed suit. Her legs, only adequate when bare, were made beautiful by dark nylons. She was dressed to the teeth, and she was beautiful.

She let her ring hand find Remo's palm and leaned against him, whispering in his ear. A delicate fragrance teased Remo's nostrils, as Cynthia said: "I love you. I lost my maidenness, but I won my man."

Then she glanced back at her diamond ring. Remo continued to stare at the approaching Palisades through the bridge's guide wires. A dull, ominous dusk without a hint of sun settled on the Jersey side of the Hudson.

"If you look hard, you can see it when it's sunny sometimes," Cynthia said.

"What?"

"Lamonica Towers. It's only twelve stories, but you can see it from the bridge sometimes." She clutched his hand like a possession.

"Darling?"

"Yes," Remo said.

"Why are your hands so rough? I mean that's a funny place to have callouses." She turned his hand over. "And on the fingertips too."

"I haven't always been a writer. I've had to work with my hands." He changed the subject quickly into small talk, but his mind wasn't on it. His thoughts were of three men under a tarpaulin in the back of a parked Cadillac in Pennsylvania. They were Felton's men, and if Felton knew they were dead, he would know that Remo had done it. Remo's best hope lay in the possibility that the bodies had not yet been found. His thoughts were interrupted by Cynthia exclaiming, "Isn't it beautiful?"

They were driving around a bumpy winding boulevard that rode the top edge of the Jersey Palisades. About a half-mile before them rose the twelve-story white Lamonica Towers.

"Well, isn't it?" Cynthia insisted.

Remo grunted. Beautiful? He had been operating less than a week and had already made enough mistakes to blow the whole operation. That beautiful building would probably be his tomb.

He had killed three men, impulsively, foolishly. Killed like a child with a new set of toys he had to use. Surprise, his most vital weapon, he had squandered. After MacCleary, Felton must have suspected someone would try to reach him through his daughter. He sent those three to protect against it. And Remo had killed them. Even if the bodies had not yet been found, the failure of the three men to report back to Felton might

156

have already triggered his nervous warning system.

Remo should have taken the money from the three men and gone directly to Lamonica Towers with it, professing love for Cynthia and asking Felton if he had sent the three men. That would have been his entrance and Felton would not have been ready for an attack.

Remo looked left, into the dark mist settling over New York Harbor. Felton must have his defenses set now. The minute Remo left Felton's daughter, even for a package of cigarettes in a store, Felton would be on him. A man who would so strenuously protect his daughter's hymen would not scar her memory with her suitor's blood. As long as he was with Cynthia, Remo was safe. But when he left . . .

"I love you too," Cynthia said.

"What?"

"You just squeezed my hand. And I said I love you too."

"Yes. Of course. I love you." Remo squeezed her soft hand again. If he could use Cynthia as a shield, right up until he got Felton alone, got him where he could get a lead to Maxwell, maybe he had a chance.

"Darling," Cynthia interrupted his thoughts.

"Yes."

"My hand. You're hurting it."

"Oh. Sorry, honey." Remo crossed his arms in front of his chest as he had seen Chiun do many times. He felt a thin smile capture his lips. Chiun had a saying for this situation, in his sing-song Oriental manner: "Poor situation is a situation of the mind. There are two sides and until the encounter is terminated, there is no such thing as a poor position to a man who can think for both sides."

It had seemed foolish when Chiun, his parchment face wrinkling slightly, had repeated it over and over. But now it made sense. If Felton could not kill him with Cynthia present, it was Felton who would be helpless, Remo who had the first move. And if he found it impossible to get Felton alone without henchmen protecting him, he could always ask for a father and son chat with Cynthia present. Remo could do it away from the Towers where the walls moved and no one could really be sure he was alone. And Cynthia might be able to support his request to keep Felton's servants and henchmen out of it.

Remo could suggest a dinner at a restaurant. Cynthia had a wild liking for eating out. Of course, as a witness, she would have to be eliminated. CURE disapproved of witnesses.

Remo suddenly noticed Cynthia was staring hard at him as if sensing something. He blanked his mind with metered breathing lest an emotional answer to a question he was sure would come would ruin everything. Chiun had once said: "Women and cows both sense rain and danger."

"You look so strange, darling," Cynthia said. Her voice had a chill edge to it. Her head was cocked as if seeing a new stroke in an old painting.

"Just nervous about meeting your father, I guess," Remo said, softly brushing her shoulder with his as he moved, dominating, close to her, keeping her blue eyes trapped in his stare. He kissed her and whispered, "No matter how it goes, I love you."

"Don't be silly," Cynthia said. "Daddy will just love you. He'll have to, when he sees how happy I am. I am happy. I feel beautiful and lovely and wanted. I never thought I'd feel this way ever."

Cynthia was wiping the lipstick smears from his lips when the cab stopped at Lamonica Towers.

"Well, honey, let's meet your father," Remo said.

"You'll love Daddy," Cynthia said. "He's really very understanding. Why, when I phoned from Philadelphia and told him he was going to meet his future son-in-law, he was really pleased. 'Bring him right over,' he said. 'I want to meet him very badly.' "

"Did he really say that?"

"His exact words." She mimicked her father's voice. "I want to meet him very badly."

An alarm bell rang in Remo's mind. Felton sounded just a bit too eager. He chuckled.

158

"Why are you laughing?"

"Nothing. It's kind of an inside joke, between myself and me."

"I hate inside jokes when I'm not inside."

"It's not a very nice inside to be on," he said.

They left the cab, Remo escorting Cynthia onto the sidewalk.

The doorman did not recognize her and was startled when she said, "Hi, Charlie."

He blinked and said, "Oh, Miss Cynthia. I thought you were still at school."

"No, I'm not," Cynthia said pleasantly and unnecessarily. The foyer was spacious and striking, with light and free-flowing modern designs interplaying in a harmony of colors and motion.

The foyer rug was soft but not too pliant and Remo felt as if he were walking over densely packed fresh-cut grass. The air was pure, too, as invisible air conditioners pumped in their charcoal-filtered product.

"No, not those elevators," Cynthia said. "We have a special one. It's in back."

"Oh, I should have guessed," Remo said.

"You're mad at something."

"No," he said. "Not at all."

"You are."

"I'm not."

"You didn't think we had this much money and you're mad because you've suddenly found out I'm stinking rich."

"Why should I be mad at that?"

"Because you think it compromises you, makes you look like a fortune-hunter."

Remo would settle for her explanation. "Well . . ." he said.

"Let's not discuss it," Cynthia said, reaching into her purse for keys. As women often do, she had argued both sides and was angry because one of them had lost.

"Now, listen," Remo said, his voice rising. "You started . . ."

"See, I told you you were mad."

"I'm not mad, dammit, but I'm going to be," Remo yelled.

Softly Cynthia said, "Then why are you yelling?"

She didn't expect an answer. She fumbled in her purse and came out with a special key on a silver chain. The key, instead of being stamped from flat metal, ended with a round tube which she inserted in a round hole on the side of the highly-burnished steel elevator door. Remo had seen the key before. He had taken one like it among the others from the ignition of a Cadillac in which three men were killed.

Cynthia held the key to the right for about ten seconds, then turned it to the left for another ten, then removed it. The elevator door opened like none Remo had ever seen before. It didn't pull to the side. It lifted up into the wall.

"You're probably thinking there's something strange about this elevator," she said.

"Sort of," Remo admitted.

"Well, Daddy goes to these weird extremes to keep undesirable elements out of the building and especially our apartment. If he's not expecting you, you have to use the key. This elevator goes only to our floor. By using this one, we don't have to wait in the room."

"Room?" Remo asked.

"Yes. A special room you have to wait in while Jimmy, the butler, looks through a one-way mirror to see who you are. I watched him once when I was little."

She placed her ringed finger on Remo's broad chest. He felt the soft, urgent pressure. "Please don't think Daddy eccentric. He's had such a hard time since mother."

"What happened?"

"Well, you'll have to know sooner or later." The elevator door shut behind them and they rose, slowly at first, then quickly, silently, cables and gears immaculately meshing in a smooth concert of action.

"Mother," Cynthia said, "carried on with another man. I was about eight. We were never close, Mother

160

and I. She worried more about how she looked than how she acted. Anyhow, Daddy found her one day with a man. I was in the living room. He told both of them to leave and they left. And we never saw them again. Since then, he hasn't been the same. I think that's why he's so protective where I'm concerned."

"You mean, he installed all these special safety gadgets after that?"

Cynthia paused. "Well, no, not exactly. He had all that as long as I could remember. But, well, he was always sensitive, and that just made him more so. Don't think badly of him. I love him."

"I have the greatest respect for him," Remo said, and then very casually added in an even tone, a very even tone: "Maxwell."

"What?"

"Maxwell."

"What?" Cynthia looked puzzled.

"I thought you said Maxwell," Remo said. "Didn't you say that?"

"No. I thought you said it."

"Said what?" Remo asked.

"Maxwell."

"I never heard of any Maxwell, have you?"

Cynthia shook her head and smiled. "Just a coffee and a car. I don't know how we got started on this."

"Neither do I," said Remo with a shrug of his shoulders. The gambit had worked but it had produced nothing.

In Folcroft classes, an instructor had made him practice dropping a name or a test word at the end of a sentence. Remo had told the instructor it was the stupidest thing he had ever heard of next to asking a man if he were a spy.

And the instructor had answered that he should try asking that very thing sometime, very casually, as if requesting a match and see what happened. "Watch the eyes," the instructor had intoned.

Remo had watched Cynthia's eyes and they had remained blue, clear, beautiful and guileless.

161

The elevator door opened, this time from the bottom, sinking out of sight. Cynthia gave a "What-can-you-do-with-Daddy?" shrug and walked into a large library, magnificently furnished in fine oak with a view of New York from a large white-tiled patio with a mended palm pot in the corner.

"This is it," Cynthia beamed, "Isn't it beautiful?"

Remo examined the walls, his eyes searching for cracks, a change in shade of paint, a bookcase out of line, a hint, any hint to where the walls moved. Nothing.

"Yes," he said, "very beautiful."

"Daddy," she yelled, "I'm home and he's with me."

Remo walked to the center of the room, keeping his back equi distant from the three walls. He suddenly wished he had brought a revolver.

The elevator door rose silently to the top, sealing off the lift. It blended almost perfectly with the white wall, the only one free of books. If he hadn't known the elevator was there, Remo never would have seen the seam. That's what MacCleary had meant by moving walls. Near the invisible elevator door was a real door, probably the one leading to the main elevator. It was arranged so a man hiding behind that door would be duck soup for someone coming off the hidden elevator.

So the walls moved.

"In the library, Daddy. We used the special elevator," Cynthia called out.

"Coming, dear." The voice was heavy.

Felton came into the room through the obvious door. Remo sized him up. Medium sized, but heavy set, with a massive neck. He wore a gray suit and he was carrying a side arm under the jacket. It was probably one of the finest jobs of concealing a shoulder holster Remo had ever seen. The suit's shoulders were padded heavily to leave a drape over the chest. Concealed under this drape on the left side was a revolver.

Remo was looking so intently for the gun that he didn't see Felton's mouth open in astonishment.

"What?" Felton yelled.

162

Startled, Remo spun quickly, moving into a defensive position on the balls of his feet. But Felton had not yelled at Remo. He was yelling at Cynthia, his bull neck turning red.

"What have you done to yourself? What have you done?"

"But, Daddy," Cynthia whined, running to the large man and throwing her arms over his powerful shoulders, "I look beautiful this way."

"You look like a street walker. You look beautiful without lipstick."

"I don't look like a street walker. I know what street walkers look like."

"You what?" Felton boomed. He raised an arm. Cynthia covered her face with her hands. Remo fought back an instinct to intervene. He just watched, carefully judging Felton. This was a good moment to examine his opponent's moves and search for the "precede", the tell-tale indication that all men had that gave away their intentions.

And Felton had one. The moment before he had raised his voice the second time, his right hand had nervously shot to the back of his head to pat down an invisible cowlick. It might have been just nervousness, but it had all the earmarks of a giveaway. Remo would watch for it.

Felton waited, his large hand poised above his head. Cynthia was trembling. More than she had to, Remo sensed.

Felton lowered the hand. "I wasn't going to hit you, dearest," he said in a pleading voice.

Cynthia trembled some more, and Remo knew she was rubbing it in; knew she had her father right where she wanted him and she wasn't going to let him off the hook until she got what she wanted.

"I wasn't going to hit you," Felton said again. "I haven't hit you since you were eight and ran away once."

"Go ahead, hit me. Hit me if it will make you feel better. Hit your only daughter."

"Dear, I wasn't."

She straightened up and lowered her hands to her hips. "And making a scene in front of my fiance, the first time you meet him. He must think we're just grand."

"I'm sorry," Felton said. He turned to Remo with a glare that escalated into pure hate—the hate of a man who not only feared an enemy, but had been embarrassed before him as well.

Remo took one look into his eyes and he knew that the bodies in the Cadillac had been found. Felton knew.

"So good to see you," Felton said, his voice suppressing his hate. "My daughter tells me your name is Remo Cabell."

"Yes it is, sir. I'm glad to meet you. I've heard a great deal about you." Remo did not move to shake hands.

"Yes, I imagine you have," Felton said. "You'll have to excuse this little scene, but I have an aversion to lipstick. I've known too many women who use that lip paint."

"Oh, Daddy, you're such a prude."

"If you would, my dear, take off the lipstick, I would appreciate it." Felton's tone was a hard-forced moderation of a great desire to scream.

"Remo likes it that way, Daddy."

"I'm sure it makes no difference to Mr. Cabell and his presence here whether you wear face paint or not. I'm sure he'd like you better without it, wouldn't you, Mr. Cabell?"

Remo had a strong urge to needle, to demand even heavier lipstick, more mascara, beauty marks over both eyes. But he fought it down.

"I think Cynthia is beautiful with or without lipstick."

Cynthia flushed. She beamed and radiated like any woman who has been charged up with a compliment.

"I'd love to take off the lipstick, Daddy, if you take off that."

164

Felton lowered his gaze. He stepped back and like an innocent lamb, said "What?"

"You're wearing it again."

"Please, dear."

"There's no need to wear one in the house." She looked back at Remo, her beautiful neck white and smooth, catching and molding, it seemed, the light from the ceiling.

"Daddy carries a lot of money sometimes and that allows him a permit for a gun. But that isn't the real reason he carries a gun."

"No?" Remo said.

"No," Cynthia said. "He carries one . . . I hate to say it . . . because he reads so many of those trashy mystery books." She turned back to her father. "I mean it."

"I haven't worn this for ten years, dear."

"And now you must have read another one of those books that used to intrigue you so. And I thought you had changed your reading taste." She spoke with mock anger but with warmth as she snaked her hand into her father's jacket and removed a gun metal blue pistol which she held at arm's length like a smelly dead mouse.

"I'll give this to Jimmy and have him put it away where he'll know it will be safe," she said with authority.

She brushed past the hulk of the man at the doorway and left as Remo called, "Don't go now."

But she was gone and Remo was alone with Felton, a disarmed Felton to be sure, but one who could count on reinforcements from the wall that moved.

Remo felt the evening air, cold and chill, blowing from the patio onto his back. He smiled politely at Felton who now had Remo in a position where he could kill him, out of Cynthia's sight.

Felton nodded gruffly. He began to speak when, from the back of the apartment, Cynthia's voice rang out: "Uncle Marvin. Uncle Marvin, what are you doing here?"

165

"Just got to tell your father something, that's all. Got to tell him something and run."

Felton, his big shoulders hunching near his ears, his large hands finding the side of the oaken desk behind him, his backside leaning on the polished desk top, looked at Remo.

"That's Marvin Moesher, not really an uncle, but he works for me. He's close to Cynthia." Felton's tone to Remo was almost conspiratorial.

"What sort of work are you in?" Remo asked.

"I have many interests. I guess you must too." Felton did not remove his eyes from Remo as a fat, thick-featured, balding man waddled into the room.

"A new employee?" Moesher asked.

Felton shook his head, but the eyes remained fixed.

"I got something private I should tell."

"Oh, I think we can talk fairly freely in front of this young man. He's very interested in our business. He might like to see our Jersey City operation." Felton brushed back an imaginary cowlick.

That was the indicator, Remo thought.

"Would you like to see it?" Felton asked.

"Not really now," Remo said, "We were all going to have dinner soon. That's what Cynthia was planning."

"You could be back in a half hour."

Moesher agreed. "A half hour, what's a half hour?" he said, with a shrug of his shoulders and a tone of voice indicating that a half hour was the most worthless unit of time imaginable. "A half hour," he repeated.

"I'd rather have dinner first," Remo said.

Felton's steely eyes fixed Remo's again. "Mr. Moesher has been on vacation. He's just come back from Folcroft Sanitarium in Rye, New York."

Don't move. Control breath. Blank mind. No show of emotion. Remo made a great display of concern for a place to sit.

He chose one of the chairs near where Felton leaned on the desk.

"He found it interesting, right, Marvin?"

"Oh," Remo said, "Is it a rest home or something?"

166

"No," Moesher said.

"What is it?" Remo asked.

"I think it may be what I thought it was," Moesher said and Felton nodded.

"What did you think it was?" Remo said.

"A sanitarium," Moesher said. "And I got some very interesting things to say about it."

Remo rose from the chair. "Good," he said. "Maybe I will take that trip to your Jersey City operation, Mr. Felton. Cynthia will probably be all night, anyway. And we can talk about this sanitarium."

Felton said to Moesher. "I can't go just now, Marvin. You take him. I'll hear from you later about your wonderful rest at Folcroft."

Felton's right hand raced along underneath the ledge of the desk and pressed a hidden button.

The secret elevator door silently lowered.

Felton yelled quickly: "Good to see you here, James. We wondered when you would get back from the store." It was an obvious signal to the man dressed in butler's uniform who stepped from the secret elevator. He had been listening to Felton and Remo and Moesher, just waiting to be called on. The butler said "Very good, sir," and walked to the other end of the room, trying to look busy.

"Marv. Take Mr. Cabell down on this elevator. It goes right to the underground garage."

As Remo moved toward the elevator with Moesher, he sized up the rawboned butler who had passed him. He was tall and rangy and also wore a concealed pistol. His was under the armpit of the waistcoat.

Remo was glad to enter the elevator first. His back was to the elevator wall, a wall that he hoped did not also move.

There were only three buttons on the main panel, PH for penthouse, one marked M, probably for the main floor, and another marked B, apparently for basement. Or was there a special basement for people like Remo?

Moesher nodded to Felton and the elevator door closed upward. Moesher was a good four inches shorter than Remo, his neck flowed in layers to his gaudy, shiny, brown suit.

He pressed one of his fat fingers against the button marked B, then turned around. "The car is in the special garage in the basement," he said.

"What kind of car is it?" Remo asked. "A Maxwell?"

The fat man slid a hand toward his gaudy jacket in one of the sloppiest giveaways Remo had ever seen. Remo could see the tension creep into the thick skull at the mention of Maxwell.

The tub turned around slowly, moving the hand from his jacket. The hand was empty. He smiled, a thick-lipped smile.

"No," he said flatly, "It's a Cadillac."

Remo nodded. "Nice car. I was riding in one last night."

The squat man nodded, but said nothing. He showed all the characteristics of a man about to kill, almost like a text book.

He could have been used as a demonstration model. He avoided the eyes of his victim, shuffled nervously, had difficulty carrying on a conversation. Remo knew what would happen. A gun brought out, aimed and silently fired. It would be soon. Beads of perspiration held a convention on the folds of the tub's forehead.

And Remo had to go with him, at least until they got off this damned elevator that might be wired for sound or television or poison gas. He had to go with Moesher until they were alone and he could try to get a lead on Maxwell from him.

Remo took an up-and-down look at Moesher. This tub of chicken fat, he thought, will be easy. Remo couldn't envision the little blob with the downcast eyes doing anything competently.

He couldn't envision it until the elevator door had opened and they had both stepped out into an underground parking garage. There were no windows and Remo could not see where the door was. The sole light in the area cast more of a gray pall than brightness

168

over a pearl gray Rolls Royce and a black Cadillac.

By the time Remo could envision Moesher doing anything right, it was too late and Remo realized he had made the cardinal mistake. He had violated the first rule beaten into him at Folcroft: pride. Never think you're so good that you can't be beaten.

Proverbs were of little use to him now as he stared down the silencer-encased muzzle of a luger held at arm's length in the pudgy fingers of Moesher. And now the brown eyes were staring at him and the feet were no longer shuffling.

The hand was steady, too. And Moesher had chosen the proper distance. Twelve feet—close enough for extreme accuracy, far enough to prevent lunges.

The little tub had moved so silently and smoothly and Remo had been so confident, that now Remo was just a squeeze away from a muzzle flash, then death.

The only picture Remo's mind could conjure up was one of Chiun, moving sideways, crabwise, skittering to escape Remo's deadly hail of bullets in the gymnasium that first day. They had discussed the technique but Remo's training was cut too short to give him mastery of it.

Moesher spoke: "Okay, booby. Where you from? Who sent you?"

Remo could have answered smart, could have fired off a sharp remark. He could have done that and been dead. But as the heavy dank basement air seemed to freeze his lungs and his hands grew damp and his eyes clouded with a film that only pressured terror could bring, he decided to play it by the book. Do what he had been instructed to do.

"What's the gun for?" he said, surprised. He moved forward, slowly, a half shuffle as the action of his hands rising over his head hid his move.

"I'm going to tell Mr. Felton about this," Remo said, still conveying fear. He waved his hands again over his head, this time taking a full step.

"Another step and you die," Moesher said. The gun didn't wobble.

169

"I come from Maxwell," Remo said.

"Who's Maxwell?" Moesher smiled.

"Kill me and you're never going to find out. Not until he comes for you himself."

It was a bluff and Moesher wasn't buying. Remo saw the brown eyes squint and knew a shot, a silent dead missile, would explode from the barrel. Now. Complete collapse of the muscles was the fastest way.

Zap went the gun and Remo's sturdy frame crumbled to the garage's cement floor. The body lay there not moving and Moesher, not quite sure whether Remo started to fall before he was hit, came closer to put a bullet in the brain. He came forward two waddling steps, raised the gun slowly and aimed at the young man's left ear. He came one step too close.

He squeezed the trigger but the ear was no longer there. One moment the body had been still, the next moment it was in the air. Remo's foot kicked Moesher's gun arm away. He fired twice but the bullets thudded against the ceiling, chipping cement like an explosion of gravel.

Remo was on Moesher's back, his left arm hooked under the fat man's armpit for leverage against the thick neck. His right arm pressed his opponent's right arm upwards until the luger dropped.

Remo concentrated the pressure, then whispered into the nearest ear: "Maxwell. Who's Maxwell?"

The tub grunted a curse. He struggled to twist his neck free. Remo was surprised how easy it was. When he was a policeman, he had never been able to use the hold competently. But the police had never taught about sustained pressures in their cursory six-week training course.

"Maxwell. Where is he?"

"Aaaah."

The tub struggled. Remo increased pressure from his left hand, down, down, down. Crack! The spinal column gave. Moesher went limp. Remo gave a final thrust. The head merely went further down in a ghastly limp compliance.

170

So Moesher wouldn't talk either. Remo stood up and let the body fall. It had been too close. Overconfidence could kill.

Moesher's thick lips opened as a trickle of blood flowed down his left cheek. His open brown eyes were dazed, clouded by death, seeing nothing.

He couldn't be left there.

Remo looked around and saw only the cars in which to hide a body. They wouldn't do. It might be embarrassing later to have to explain what happened to dear old Uncle Marvin, if he and Cynthia got into that car.

He saw a door in the corner of the garage enclosure. He walked to it. Inside was a large commercial washer and dryer, apparently for the use of Lamonica Towers' residents. Remo glanced at the dryer, white and spotless in the corner. A cruel smile formed on his lips.

He dragged Moesher's heavy body across the garage floor to the dryer and with one hand flipped open the door. The body was big but the opening for clothes was twenty-four inches in diameter, big enough for even a big body. Remo stuffed Moesher's head and shoulders into the dryer compartment, twisted them until they turned sideways, making room for the rest of the body. He pushed Moesher's legs in. He noticed he wore argyle socks. With a snap of his fingernails, he opened an artery on Moesher's neck. Then he dried his hands on Moesher's trousers.

He snapped shut the glass-fronted round door and looked for the starter button. "That cheap bastard, Felton," he murmured. "A coin machine. For people who live in his apartment building."

He reached for his pocket, then said to hell with it. He wasn't going to feed his own money into Felton's goddam laundry.

Remo opened the round door again and reached far into the machine until he felt pockets. He reached in and yanked out all Moesher's change. Good. He had a lot of dimes.

Remo clicked the door shut again, then placed six

dimes in the coin slot. The machine groaned into operation, the cylinder spinning, the heat increasing. Remo pocketed the remaining quarter and three pennies, then stepped back and watched the accelerating swirl of clothes and flesh.

A pink film clouded the round window. That was the blood. The centrifugal force of the spinning cylinder would force the blood from Moesher's body through the cut artery. The heat would dry him out and for sixty cents, Moesher was well on his way to becoming a mummy.

"Oh, Remo, you're a bastard," Remo said softly to himself. He whistled as he walked back toward the elevator. Now to get back to the twelfth floor.

CHAPTER THIRTY-THREE

The private elevator door offered the same type of lock it had on the main floor. Remo reached into his jacket pocket for the keys he had taken from the driver the night before. He glanced back at the garage and saw the Luger.

Remo trotted back to where he had overcome Moesher on the cement floor. He picked up the black gun. Did he need it? Felton would have no doubts about what had happened to Moesher. There would be no reason not to carry the gun now.

Remo fingered the hard black handle with sweat grip. MacCleary had always said: "Don't listen to everything Chiun tells you about guns. They're still good. Carry one and use one."

And Chiun, when Remo had finally talked to him later, had maintained that guns spoiled the art.

Remo glanced at the barrel, dull, gunmetal blue. Chiun was over seventy years old, MacCleary was decomposing. Remo flipped the gun into a dark corner. Weapons really did take the fun out of it all.

The tubular key, first to the right, then to the left, worked in the elevator door.

Remo pushed the button marked PH. Riding up, he straightened his jacket, wrinkled in the scuffle below. He tightened his tie and in the burnished button panel with only three stops, saw enough of the outline of his head to straighten his hair.

The elevator stopped but the door didn't open. Of course, Remo thought, there was some kind of button to open it. He had ignored what Cynthia had done earlier to open it.

He examined the panel again. Three buttons. Nothing else. His eyes roamed the door, the metal

173

door. Nothing. Back to the panel. He was about to push his hand against the entire door panel to see if it opened by slight pressure, when voices drifted toward the car.

The elevator had been constructed so that a person standing in it when it was at the penthouse level could hear signal commands from the library. Remo hesitated. It was Cynthia's voice. She was protesting. "He is not like that at all. He loves me."

Felton's voice: "Then why did he take the one thousand dollars I offered him?"

"I don't know. I don't know what you told him, or even if you threatened him."

"Don't be silly, my dear. He took the money because I told him he would get no more if he married you. He was only after your money, dearest. I was protecting you. Could you imagine what would have happened if you had married him and then found out what he was like? When he took the money, I told Uncle Marvin to take him down and put him on a bus."

"I don't care. I love him." Cynthia was sobbing.

Remo did not want to have to tell Felton he was a liar just yet, not in front of Cynthia. Plenty of time for that later. He took out his wallet and leafed through the bills. He had about one thousand two hundred dollars. Smith would have a heart attack.

He rolled up one thousand dollars into a wad and replaced his wallet. He pushed the door's face, and as he guessed, it slid downward and he stepped into the library.

Felton looked as if he had just been kicked in the stomach by a mule; Cynthia as if she had received a reprieve from the chair.

Remo hurled the one thousand dollars on the rug and, forcing himself not to laugh, announced grandly: "I love Cynthia. Not your filthy lucre."

"Remo, darling," Cynthia cried, running to him. She threw her arms around his neck and violently kissed his cheeks and lips. Remo stared at Felton through the barrage of affection.

174

Felton was visibly shaken. He could only return Remo's stare, then blurted out: "Moesher? Where's Moesher?"

"He was going to put me on the bus. Then he decided to go for a spin by himself." Remo smiled, a smile that was immediately smothered in warm searching lips.

Felton had regained his composure by dinner. They ate by candlelight. James, the butler, served. Felton said it was the maid's night off and he had personally prepared the meal. Remo responded he was overcome by an upset stomach and could not eat a bite.

The preliminaries were over. Both men knew that. And each knew that the only thing left was a showdown between them—a personal showdown. They would both know when the time for that had come. And this was not it. The dinner was like the Christmas Day armistice on the battlefield and Felton played the role of the proud father.

"Cynthia has probably told you we're very wealthy," he said to Remo. "Did she tell you how I made my money?"

"No, she didn't. I'd be interested in knowing."

"I'm a junkman."

Remo smiled politely. Cynthia sputtered, "Oh, Daddy."

"It's true, my dear. Every penny we have today is from the junk business." He seemed determined to tell his story and launched into it without urging.

"Americans, Mr. Cabell, are the world's most prolific producers of junk. They annually throw away many millions of dollars of quite good and quite usable merchandise because buying new things is almost a psychological compulsion with them."

"Like a homicidal maniac or a pathological liar," Remo offered helpfully.

Felton ignored the interruption.

"I first noticed this during the war years. How Americans, even faced with shortages, would throw away many products which still had a long life

175

expectancy. In a small way, I capitalized on it. I scraped together every dollar I could and bought a junkyard.

"Have you ever been in a junkyard, Mr. Cabell, to buy something? It is impossible. There may be hundreds of what you want around, but no one knows where to find them.

"I decided to bring some organization to the junk business. I hired specialists to supervise the operations. One crew did nothing but buy and recondition old washing machines and clothes dryers. A perfectly good washing machine could be bought as junk for five dollars. We'd fix it until it was as good as new. But instead of selling it back to a private buyer, we put it to work for us. Through the forties, I opened more than seventy-five automatic laundries throughout the metropolitan area—all of them outfitted with junked washing machines and dryers. Because I had no large investment in equipment, I could charge less than any of my competitors. Everytime I heard of a new laundromat opening somewhere, I moved in my junk machinery and opened as near to him as possible. By undercutting his prices, I could put him out of business. Then as he liquidated, I could buy his brand new equipment for a song. This proved very profitable."

Felton smiled. "That may sound particularly vicious and cruel to you, Mr. Cabell. But this is a vicious and cruel world."

"I've noticed," Remo said. Felton went on:

"With junked automobiles, I also feel I have made some contributions to our economy. Perhaps that is a foolish attitude, but each man thinks that what he does is important.

"I operate an auto junkyard in Jersey City. It is the largest junkyard in the world. It is also, so far as I can tell, the only one that is as organized as a department store.

"We roll in a junked car that we have bought for only a few dollars. The car may have been almost totally smashed in an accident, but it's surprising how much remains after even a total loss. The car is moved from section to section of the yard. Usable fenders are removed; windows are taken out; seats are taken out in another section; so are such items as steering wheels and headlights and doors. Each of these items is carefully compartmented, and I would daresay that if you went to this yard and asked for a rear door and trunk handle to a 1939 Plymouth, my men would have it for you in less than five minutes. Of course, for this kind of service, we can charge premium rates."

Remo nodded and smiled. "Do you think you might have something in stock for my 1934 Maxwell?"

Before Felton could say anything, Cynthia said: "There you go with that silly Maxwell business again."

Felton looked at Cynthia coldly. To Remo, he said: "I don't know if we would have any parts for your Maxwell. Perhaps you'd like to drive down there with me and see?"

Remo agreed with alacrity, despite Cynthia's protest that they should all spend the night together, getting acquainted.

"No, dear," Felton said. "It would be a chance for Mr. Cabell and me to have a father-and-son talk."

Felton dropped his fork when Remo said: "He's right, dear, we should have a talk alone. And since we're going to be such close friends, perhaps I can even persuade him to call me Remo."

Remo smiled, a good-son smile, and Felton, who had matched Cynthia's prodigious eating ability through the meal, decided he was too full for dessert. Jimmy, the butler, said gruffly, "Shall I remove the plates?"

He had stared at Remo all during the meal, hating him for killing Scottichio and Moesher and, at one time, Remo thought he detected the welling up of a tear in the corner of Jimmy's eye.

"Life is rough," he whispered to the butler. He got no answer.

"I don't feel like dessert," Felton said again.

177

Cynthia slammed down a spoon. Her beautiful face twisted into a childlike rage. "Well, damn it, I do."

"But, darling," Remo said.

"But darling crap," said the Briarcliff philosophy student.

Felton blinked. "What language!"

"Language, hell. You're not leaving me here."

Jimmy tried to soothe the girl as an old friend. He didn't get a word out of his mouth. His lips parted and Cynthia yelled: "You shut up, too."

"Dear," Remo said.

"If anyone goes, we all go. That's it."

Remo leaned back in his chair, playing with the rim of the full plate. Cynthia had gotten bitchy. All right. Fine. He needed a shield. As long as she was with him, Felton would do nothing.

He glanced at the glowering hulk of a man dominating the end of the table. Or would he?

Cynthia had her way. The four of them rode silently down in the private elevator to the basement where they climbed into the Rolls. Remo listened for, but didn't hear, the dryer. Sixty cents didn't go too far nowadays, he thought.

Jimmy drove, Felton sat beside him and Cynthia leaned on Remo in the rear. Before clambering into the car, Felton had peeked in through the window of the black Cadillac, looking for Moesher.

Cynthia kept kissing Remo playfully. Remo could see Felton watching them in the rear-view mirror, his brow wrinkling at every brush of Cynthia's lips against Remo's cheeks.

"You know," she whispered. "I've never seen the Jersey City yard. I'm kind of interested, too. I love you."

"I love you, too," Remo said, staring at the back of her father's head. He could kill them both now. Easy. But Maxwell. They were his lead to Maxwell.

The car bounced along Kennedy Boulevard. The rutted disgrace that was called the county's main

178

thoroughfare. They rolled past slums, past patches of neat two-story buildings, past brightly lit used car lots, into Journal Square, the hub of Jersey City.

At Communipaw Avenue, the car turned right. More dingy buildings, more used car lots, then the car wheeled left, down Route 440.

"We're almost there," Felton said.

CHAPTER THIRTY-FOUR

The car sped along Route 440, suddenly bare of construction. Then, a right turn, and they were on a gravel road, bouncing along in a sudden enveloping darkness.

The car stopped at a corrugated steel gate. The headlights played on a triangular yellow sign which read: "Protected by Romb Detective Agency."

The lights went out. Remo heard crickets in the distance. "We're here," Felton said.

Remo said a silent prayer to one of Chiun's thousands of gods. "Vishnu, preserve me."

He opened the car door and stepped out onto the hard gravel. It made a crunch. The nearby river air bathed him in a chill. The night stars were clouded over. He smelled a faint odor of burnt coffee coming from somewhere. He rubbed his hands.

Behind him, he heard Felton warn his daughter that there were many rats in the areas. Did she want to come? No, she decided. She'd stay in the car. "Keep the windows closed," he suggested.

The doors opened again, then closed.

"Let's go," Felton said advancing on the gate. The butler grunted assent. Remo knew they were both armed.

"Yeah," Remo said. "Let's go."

Felton unlocked the gate and opened it. It groaned, like metal abused by the weather. Remo tried to linger, to be last. But they waited.

"After you," Felton said.

"Thank you," Remo answered.

They walked down the gravel road, Felton in front, Jimmy behind, Remo in the center. Felton went through the motions of explaining the yard's operation,

180

and pointed out where different car parts for different years and different makes were stored.

The crunch of their footsteps sounded like an army advancing. Remo could not see Jimmy, but he sure as hell could look at the back of the head in front of him. Felton wore no hat.

On they marched, through the night, down the road. Remo heard water rippling nearby, the lights pulsing off the river.

The minute Felton's hand went to the back of his head in his giveaway gesture, Remo would move. That was all the leeway he could give.

A dark hulk of a concrete structure loomed ahead like a giant pillbox by the sea.

"That's the heart of our operation," Felton said. Remo moved closer. The pillbox had a concrete ribbon of road leading down an incline into it. A dilapidated car was parked on the ribbon, blocks under the wheels.

"When we finish stripping a car, what's left goes into this processor and out comes a cube of scrap iron that we sell to the steel mills. We made a lot of money during the war, didn't we, Jimmy?"

"Yeah," Jimmy said. He was close behind Remo.

"This is where . . ." Felton's hand went to the back of his head . . . "where we keep our Maxwells! Now!"

Remo leaned forward as the slow lazy blow came from the butler. He pulled with it like child's play and crumpled to the ground.

No overconfidence. See what they do. Maybe Maxwell is here.

"Nice hit, Jimmy. I think we got the bastard. We finally got him."

Remo saw Felton's highly polished black shoes move near his lips. Then he felt a sharp crack on his chin. Felton had kicked him.

He did not move.

"I think you killed him." Felton said. "What'd you hit him with?"

"My hand, boss. I still didn't get a good shot at him."

"He's the one," Felton said, with resignation. "He got Scottichio and Moesher."

"I wish he'd a lived to go in the machine."

Felton shrugged. "I feel tired, Jimmy. I don't care anymore. Get him ready."

Remo felt Jimmy's large bony hands reach around his rib cage and hoist. He was dragged, his feet scraping, around to the ramp end of the concrete blockhouse. Through half-opened eyes he saw Felton walk to the other end of the building.

The junk car's doors were off and Jimmy rested Remo on his bony knee for a moment, then threw him headfirst onto the floor mat where the front seat had been. Remo heard engines, not car engines, groan. Jimmy removed a block from in front of the car's front right wheel. Walking toward the back of the car, he leaned in to throw one last punch. Remo Williams had waited long enough.

With his left hand he grabbed the large bony wrist and snapped it, silently, swiftly. Jimmy would have screamed if Remo's right hand had not buried itself knuckle-deep into his solar plexis, only a split-second earlier, knocking the air and the sound from him. Remo smashed the nose bone with his left hand and Jimmy went out.

Remo slid out from under Jimmy's limp frame, then pushed Jimmy into the car, in the place intended for Remo. Remo trotted silently to the back of the car and removed another block from behind the rear wheel.

The engines that Remo had heard groaned louder, and at the bottom of the concrete ramp, a steel door rose on hydraulic pistons. It opened a steel compartment that in the dim light Remo could see was big enough for several cars at once.

Remo released the emergency brake in the car, gave it a push, then sat on Jimmy's head and gently eased the car down the hill into the giant box.

As the car bumped to a halt against the end wall, Remo dashed for freedom. He almost stumbled as he heard the giant steel door slowly lowering with a hideous hiss.

Remo heard sounds from the other end of the giant concrete pillbox. He moved silently on the balls of his feet, like a phantom gliding over a padded graveyard.

Peering around the wall, he saw Felton, stripped to his white shirt, his coat and jacket lying on the ground, sweating over an instrument panel.

Felton yelled: "Everything all right, Jimmy? You got him set?"

Remo stepped around the building. "I'm all set, Felton. All set."

Felton went for the gun. With one swift motion, Remo snapped the revolver from his hand. He moved behind Felton, and spun him wildly around in a circle, moving him like a rolling barrel along the concrete sidewalk beside the concrete and steel crusher.

It was like dribbling a basketball. Felton's blows were wild and thrashing. He was too old for this business, too old.

By the time Remo got Felton to the other end, the steel door had closed. Felton spun around and swung. Remo caught the blow on his left arm and crumbled Felton with a soft chop to the temple.

Felton collapsed to the concrete. And Remo saw something sticking out beneath the steel door. It was a leg. Jimmy had tried to slide out. He hadn't made it. The steel door had sliced it like a hot wire going through cheese. The tip of the shoe seemed to be jerking, not from impulses which were severed, but like an organism, primeval without intellect.

Remo gave Felton another tap on the temple, then went back to the control panel. It was a simple panel but Remo didn't understand it.

There was a right lever with gradations, a forward lever, a top lever, an entrance lever, and an automatic control.

Remo grabbed the entrance lever. Then it hit him like a jolt of electricity. He began to laugh. He was still laughing as he heard the heavy steel door begin to hiss open.

He picked up Felton's pistol, then walked to the ramp at the other end of the concrete blockhouse. "Maxwell," he kept repeating. "Maxwell." Felton was where he had left him, his arms spread grotesquely wide over the concrete driveway.

Jimmy had rolled back down the incline after the door had severed his leg. But the hiss of the opening door drove him on. With his one leg and a stump and two hands, Jimmy was hopping and crawling like a horrible, crippled, crab up the incline, trying to escape. In the faint moonlight, Remo could see the terror etched deeply into his face.

Remo cocked Felton's pistol and fired a bullet calmly into Jimmy's one good leg. The bullet spun Jimmy around and Remo took a step into the driveway and kicked the big Texan back into the box over the leg that was no longer his.

Then Remo lifted Felton and heaved him down the concrete incline. Remo ran around to the controls and pushed back the entrance lever. The heavy steel door hissed shut again and a light went on inside the blockhouse. Through some sort of heavy plastic peephole, Remo could see inside. Felton was not moving. Nor was Jimmy.

Felton would come to soon enough. Remo reached into his shirt pocket and lit a cigarette. He glanced once more at the control panel, mumbled "Maxwell" again with a smile, and settled down to smoking his cigarette. So that was it.

On the fourth puff, he heard a scratching on the plastic shield. He took a deliberately long time turning around. When he did, there was Felton's face, pressed against the plastic window.

The old man's hair was wild. He was yelling something. Remo could not make it out.

Carefully, Remo formed the word with his lips: "Maxwell."

Felton's head shook.

"I know you don't know," Remo yelled.

Felton looked desperately puzzled.

"Here's another one," Remo yelled. "MacCleary?"

Felton shook his head.

"Don't know him either, huh?" Remo called. "I didn't think you would. He was just a guy with a hook. Think of him when you're being crushed to death. Think of him when you're a hood ornament on somebody's car. Think of him because he was my friend."

Remo turned from Felton who scratched frantically on the plastic window and examined the idiot panel. He shrugged his shoulders. He heard a muffled plea for mercy. But there had been no mercy for MacCleary or the other CURE agents or for America.

He had been created the destroyer and this was what he was meant to do. He pushed the lever marked automatic and the machine moaned into operations, its giant hydraulic presses forcing hundreds of thousands of pounds of pressure into a moving wall. And Remo knew he was not just working at a job, he was living his role in life, fulfilling what he was born for.

It took no more than five minutes. First the front wall pressed in to crush the contents of the blockhouse, then a side wall moved in to crush from another direction, then the roof slowly lowered and it was over. When all the hydraulic walls had returned to their normal positions, Remo peered through the plastic window. All he saw was a cube of metal, four feet square. An automobile and two humans, now only a cube of scrap iron.

Remo looked around for an implement. He saw a rusted crowbar resting against one of the blockhouse's exterior walls.

He walked slowly over to the crowbar, picked it up, then went back to the panel. He didn't know how to turn off the lights, let alone the machine. Someone would find the cube in the morning. It would probably be shipped out with the rest of the scrap.

Remo pried a small metal badge from the top of the

control panel. It was a trademark. It was as far as CURE's one agent had been able to penetrate.

It read: "Maxwell Steel Reducer. Maxwell Industries, Lima, O."

Cynthia didn't mind too much that Daddy had decided to stay at the yard. She wanted to be alone with Remo anyway, and she was happy that they had finally gotten to understand each other.

She didn't even mind that Daddy didn't come home for breakfast. Remo made a personal phone call from Lamonica Towers to Dr. Smith at Folcroft. He made the call from Felton's bed while Cynthia slept beside him.

"A what?" Smith said.

"That's what Maxwell was," Remo repeated. "Felton was the boss."

"Impossible."

"All right, it's impossible," Remo said.

There was a long pause.

"How much could one of them cost?"

"How should I know, damn it?"

"Just wondering," Smith said.

"Look. I know where we can get one cheap."

"Oh, really?"

"A friend of mine now owns one. She'll sell it to me cheap. One hundred billion dollars," Remo yelled into the receiver, then hung up.

He was caressing his bedmate's fanny when the phone rang.

"This is Viaselli," said the man at the other end of the receiver. "I just wanted to thank Norman for releasing my brother-in-law, Tony."

"This is Carmine Viaselli, right?" Remo asked.

"That's right. Who is this?"

"I'm an employee of Mr. Felton's and I'm glad you called."

Remo continued: "Mr. Felton called me early this morning and said I should try to reach you. He wanted to see you tonight. Something or other about a Maxwell."

186

"Where should I meet him?"

"He has a junk yard on Route 440. It's the first right off Communipaw Avenue. He'll be there."

"What time?"

"About nine o'clock." Remo felt Cynthia roll into him, cuddling her face in his chest. She slept in the raw. "Better yet, Mr. Viaselli. better make it ten o'clock."

"Right," came the voice from the phone.

Remo hung up.

"Who was it, darling?" Cynthia asked sleepily.

"A man about business."

"What business, dear?" she murmured.

"My business."

AFTERWORD

When was the last time you saw a hero? Not one of those mindless, looney-bin rejects who line the bookracks: The Exterminator, The Extincter, The Ripper, The Slasher, The Wiper-Outer, The Mutilator, The Ix-Nayer, all those same series, with their same covers, their same plots, and their same moronic machine-gunning leads who figure the best way to solve a problem is to shoot it.

No. A real life-saving, mind-craving hero for the world today.

Not Tarzan, he won't help. He's in Africa. Not Doc Savage, he was in the thirties and forties. Not James Bond. He was left behind at the turn of the decade.

For the seventies and eighties, the word is in. It's *The Destroyer*.

Why *The Destroyer*? Why the phenomenon that has writers, editors, literary agents, ad men—people who deal in words, and who you think would know better—following these tales of Remo Williams and his Korean teacher Chiun with the same kind of passion and faith that only a few like Holmes and Watson have instilled?

Why has this . . . this . . . *paperback* series drawn such high reviews from such lofty heights as *The New York Times, Penthouse, The Village Voice,* and the *Armchair Detective,* a journal for mystery fanatics?

Honesty.

Look beyond the facts that *The Destroyer* books are written very well and are very funny and very fast and very good.

The Destroyer is honest to today, to the world, and most importantly to itself.

And who is *The Destroyer*? Who is this new breed of Superman?

Just sad, funny, used-to-be-human-but-now-isn't-quite

Remo. Wise-assing Remo whose favorite line is: "That's the biz, sweetheart."

What's this? A hero who doesn't like killing? Not some crazy who massacres anything that moves with lip-smacking pleasure?

No, Remo doesn't have the callous simplicity of a machine gun to solve the world's problems. He uses his hands, his body, himself. What he's saying with "that's the biz, sweetheart" is that you knew the job of fighting evil was dangerous when you took it.

But somebody has to punish these soul corrupters, and reality has bypassed the government and the police and the media and the schools and has chosen Remo.

And who's he to argue with reality?

The other fist backing up *The Destroyer* is philosophy. Yes, that's right. Philosophy.

It isn't just the incredibly drawn supporting characters who are written so real that you see them on the street everyday. Not just the "future relevancy" of the books' strong stories, even though *The Destroyer* has beaten the media to such subjects as radical chic, world starvation, detente, and soap operas. Not only that, but *The Destroyer* gets it better with a more accurate view. Chiun was delivering the truth on soap operas long before *Time* magazine's cover story. When the literati was pounding its collective breast over the struggle of "the noble red man," Remo was up to his neck in the movement, and delivering some telling truths about "the Indians from Harlem, Harvard, and Hollywood."

No. What's different here is the philosophy of Sinanju, that forbidding village in North Korea—it's real—which spawned Chiun and the centuries of master assassins preceding him. The philosophy culled from its early history, a history of starvation and deprivation so severe that its people became killers for pay so the babies wouldn't have to be drowned in the bay.

Kind of chokes you up, doesn't it?

Chiun too. He'll tell you about it. And tell you about it. And tell you about it. And he'll tell you other things.

Chiun on Western morality:

"When a Korean comes to the end of his rope, he closes

the window and kills himself. When an American comes to the end of his rope, he opens the window and kills someone else. Hopefully, it's just another American."

Chiun on old girlfriends:

"Every five years, a white person changes. If you see her again, you will kill her in your eyes. That last remembrance of what you once loved. Wrinkles will bury it. Tiredness will smother it. In her place will be a woman. The girl dies when the woman emerges."

Chiun on Sinanju:

"Live, Remo, live. That is all I teach you. You cannot grow weak, you cannot die, you cannot grow old unless your mind lets you do it. Your mind is greater than all your strength, more powerful than all your muscles. Listen to your mind, Remo. It is saying to you: 'Live'."

Philosophy. It makes the incredible things they do, just this side of possible.

And it says that Remo and Chiun are not vacuous, cold-hearted killers. Nor are they fantasy, cardboard visitors from another planet with powers and abilities, etc., etc.

They're just two a-little-more-than-human beings.

Chiun must have been reincarnated from everybody's Jewish momma. Remo is the living embodiment of everyman, 1970s style.

Will Chiun ever stop kvetching about Remo being a pale piece of pig's ear and admit the love he feels for him?

Will Remo ever get the only thing he really wants, a home and family?

Keep reading and see. *Destroyer* today, headlines tomorrow.

Remo Williams, *The Destroyer,* didn't create the world he's living in. He's just trying to change it. The best way he know how.

And for the world's greatest assassin, that's the biz, sweetheart.

—Ric Meyers,
a still-born fetus
in the eyes of Sinanju.